After Dinner Conversation

Philosophy | Ethics Short Story Magazine

May 2024

After Dinner Conversation *Magazine* – May 2024

This magazine publishes fictional stories that explore ethical and philosophical questions in an informal manner. The purpose of these stories is to generate thoughtful discussion in an open and easily accessible manner.

Names, characters, businesses, organizations, places, events, and incidents are either the product of the author's imagination or are used fictitiously. Any resemblance to actual persons, living or dead, events, or locales is entirely coincidental. The magazine is published monthly in print and electronic format.

Vol. 5, No. 5

https://www.afterdinnerconversation.com

After Dinner Conversation believes humanity is improved by ethics and morals grounded in philosophical truth and that philosophical truth is discovered through intentional reflection and respectful debate. In order to facilitate that process, we have created a growing series of short stories across genres, a monthly magazine, and two podcasts. These accessible examples of abstract ethical and philosophical ideas are intended to draw out deeper discussions with friends, family, and students.

Table Of Contents

* * *

From the Editor

We are continually evolving, and this issue is no exception. We have added a "Special Thanks" section at the end of the magazine for financial supporters. Long story short, literary magazines have three funding legs: paid subscriptions, arts grants, and private donors. We simply couldn't exist without all three funding legs, and we are overdue in giving more public thanks to our private donors who keep us running. Of course, we hope you will consider becoming a donor as well, and we would be honored to add your name to future issues.

We have also added a "Content Disclosure" at the start of each story. Personally, I hate the idea of trigger warnings. Life doesn't give a trigger warning before it throws the proverbial car crash your way, and raising children who think it does, in my opinion, sets them up for shock. *See Old Fart vs. Society.*

That said, this PG-13(*ish*) magazine has grown into more classrooms and parent/child conversations, and I do think it is fair to give facilitators a spoiler-free heads-up on what they might expect from a story. There isn't a standardized list of content disclosures, but you can see the list we draw from on our website. We hope this will save you some time.

I also want to mention our 2024 themed book series releases are underway. Please consider giving them a look.

Kolby Granville – Editor

Disconnect

Julia Meinwald

* * *

Content Disclosure: Sexual Situations

* * *

It's 7:12 p.m., and Simone has this guy in the palm of her proverbial hand. Technically speaking, it's not her hand. The guy is on a date with Alexis, one of Simone's most loyal clients at Connect2. Simone is clicked into her terminal three miles away. Alexis has flipped the switch, giving Simone full control over her actions and words and full access to her thoughts and sensations. Each client feels different to pilot. If the client has joint pain or a headache, the pilot feels it. Many pilots find their first week on the job an almost spiritual experience, feeling the similarities and differences in how various human bodies move through the world. Simone, one of the most respected, in-demand pilots at Connect2, has inhabited over two hundred people.

Piloting Alexis is fun for Simone. Alexis has the sharpest sense of smell Simone has ever encountered, and her near-constant pulse of nervous energy feels energizing to Simone. Alexis is a well-oiled Porsche, and Simone is a racecar driver. Or something. Simone doesn't really care about cars, but Alexis has some strong memories associated with her father's prized Maserati. It's not Simone's job to unpack this. It's her job to make this guy fall for Alexis.

It doesn't hurt that Alexis is beautiful. She's gorgeous in a predictable, blonde and leggy way. She has a nice laugh, too, which Simone deploys now to show this guy that she gets his Vonnegut reference. Simone hasn't actually read Vonnegut, but she knows enough to recognize popular characters and ideas. Guys never want to talk about the books anyway. They just want to throw down the reference to see if their date picks it up. "You're funny," she says to the guy. This is a bit on the nose for Simone, but she's calculated right; the guy preens and, as if repaying a social debt, asks her about herself. Or rather, he asks her about Alexis. Or, rather, he asks "Alexis" about Alexis.

If Alexis were in control right now, she would demur. She can't stand talking about herself and honestly finds a question as broad as "Tell me about yourself" borderline aggressive. Simone, however, has no problem with this. In her own life, she can happily monologue about the flurry of worries and amusements filling any given day. It's only slightly more difficult to do this for someone else. She tells the guy about the book Alexis is reading, about Alexis's sister's impending wedding, and transitions seamlessly into a story about a business lunch that draws attention to the impressive company where Alexis works in HR. She's careful to speak in Alexis's syntax. The less successful pilots at Connect2 go too far, making their clients perfect embodiments of charm. When the client flips the switch back and tries to take over, the discrepancies are glaring, and the subsequent dates are disastrous. Connect2 estimates that close to 15 percent of first dates in Los Angeles involve a pilot, but getting caught as a passenger on a date is still considered a red flag in the dating world. The trick is to present Alexis as faithfully as possible—just amping up a few parameters to make a better first impression.

Simone has just revealed where Alexis went to college, and the guy makes a face that both women read as patronizing. Simone feels Alexis's impulse to flinch, but she stifles it. She pauses for a moment to see if Alexis is going to signal that she'd like to take control of the date, but she doesn't. Generally, clients flip the switch to take control mid-date in two situations: when they want to end the date prematurely or when they want to get physical. Every now and then, Simone gets someone who wants her to pilot the first kiss, but anything beyond that is forbidden by the Connect2 code of conduct. In Alexis and Simone's first few months together, Alexis would constantly flip the emergency override switch—forcibly seizing control against Simone's advice. A guy teasingly mocks her order? Emergency override. A guy doesn't get Simone-as-Alexis's funny joke? Uber is en route. After enough dates like this, though, Simone has earned Alexis's trust.

This guy seems judgmental, but Simone has gotten some positive bio-signals from Alexis. Part of Simone's job is to debrief with Alexis after the dates. To help her clarify her own feelings about a guy and choose a course of action. The consulting part is fun, but what Simone loves most are the dates themselves. Some of her friends think that piloting is like a superpower, but in truth, it's easier to see (and be) what someone else wants when you don't have to tend to your own personal desires. A surprising number of pilots at Connect2, including Simone, are single.

"I'm honestly shocked how many girls I go on dates with who just *don't read*," the guy is saying.

"Okay," says Simone, "I could be wrong, but is that tattoo on your wrist a literary reference?"

* * *

The day after the date is Alexis's twenty-ninth birthday. She knows it's not a big deal birthday. Next year, she might force herself to throw some sort of party for the big three-O. To pick the best, quietest, quirkiest bar in Silverlake, spend twelve hours crafting the perfect three-sentence email invite, then despair when only ten people show up and no one stays past midnight. Probably, though, she won't. Alexis doesn't act, she reacts. She receives, she waits, she happily makes the second move. It's a safer, easier way to move through the world.

Alexis doesn't list her birthday on social media, but it still feels like a personal affront that she's only gotten a handful of birthday greetings so far. None of them feel at all personal to her. She's got messages from her parents and her sister on the family text chain, but those feel rote, too. Alexis can't help but read this as a referendum on the quality of her personality. If she were smarter, funnier, kinder, she would probably be surrounded by gifts, confetti, and people who love her.

Her twenty-eighth birthday wasn't bad. Her boyfriend at the time took her to dinner, but just at their local Italian place, which had paper napkins and fewer cheese and pepper flake shakers than tables; the wait staff would ferry them back and forth between diners as needed. They talked, as they usually did, about his fantasy hockey league and how unethical and stupid various politicians were. The quotidian quality of the date made Alexis wonder if he was planning on dumping her. A few months later, he did indeed end things; Alexis was never sure if the lackluster birthday dinner was an early warning sign or not.

In an effort to celebrate herself (something culture seems to want her to do), Alexis takes a cupcake from her fridge and a birthday card from work out of her bag. All her coworkers have signed it, but the closest thing to a personalized message is the drawing of a rat wearing a party hat that her colleague Meredith drew in the card's lower right-hand corner. Meredith draws *Birthday Rat* on everyone's cards, but at least it has more personality than the usual "Happy birthday" and "Hope you have a fantabulous day!"

Her doorbell rings as she's stoically waiting for her cupcake to warm up and lose that cold fridge feeling. She springs to the door with an embarrassing dose of optimism. She's greeted by an old Asian woman bearing two dozen roses, which Alexis signs for and brings to the kitchen with cumbersome happiness. The card informs her that the roses are from Connect2. She's disappointed that they are from a company and not a person, but she has to admire their customer service.

Alexis suspects she's probably one of Connect2's most active users. She had hated dating before, but dates piloted by Simone are fun, and the debriefs are even better. Sometimes Alexis even accepts a date with a guy she knows she's not interested in, just so she can make fun of him with Simone after the fact.

Alexis's phone dings. It's an email from Simone listing

twenty-four things to love about Alexis—one for each rose in the bouquet. Alexis lifts the cupcake to her lips, reading the list again and again with each chocolaty bite.

* * *

Alexis shows up twelve minutes early for her debrief with Simone, sits in her car until she is only four minutes early, then enters the Connect2 building. The door to Simone's office is open, and Simone has implanted herself into a beanbag chair with two coffee mugs in front of her. Alexis lowers herself into the other beanbag as Simone exclaims, "Girl! You're wearing the sweater!" Simone and Alexis spent a good ten minutes going over the pros and cons of purchasing a turtleneck, debating whether Alexis could pull it off, and delving into what the larger ramifications of such a sartorial choice might be. Alexis shrugs with some pleasure.

"It looks so good!" says Simone. "You look like a stylish bunny rabbit. Can I touch it?"

Alexis nods, and Simone runs her hand down the length of Alexis's arm. To Alexis, it feels like the kinesthetic equivalent of ASMR. "Mmmmm," says Simone. "Softness."

"This is my first time wearing it," says Alexis.

"I'm honored I get to see it on its maiden voyage!" says Simone. "So, obviously, we have an agenda, but can I tell you a story first?"

"Always," says Alexis, settling into her beanbag.

"Okay, so I had an intro session with a new client yesterday. A really rich guy who just decided to open his marriage and wants to find a new sidepiece, these are his words, 'as efficiently as possible.' So, we finish up the regular intake stuff, and then he asks me... if I'll cut his hair."

"What?" Alexis laughs.

"Yeah, I was like, my dude, that is not part of this service, but best of luck to you."

"I might have done it," says Alexis, picking up the mug Simone has set out for her and inhaling deeply.

"Do you know how to cut hair?" asks Simone.

"A little. I cut some friends' hair in college. I've always thought there's something kind of romantic about it. In the right context, I mean. Something about how they trust you. It's like you're doing a loving act of service."

"Plus, you're kind of molding the person into a new version of themselves. New do, new you."

"Right. Like in those spy shows where the woman gets a new haircut and suddenly no one recognizes her."

Simone laughs. "So, shall we discuss our first order of business? Thumbs up or thumbs down on our Great Literary Mind?"

Alexis does a sideways thumb, and Simone lets out a theatrical groan. "Alexis!" she says. "They can't all be sideways thumbs! Seriously, is there *any* chance *this guy* is your soulmate?"

"There's a chance this coffee is my soulmate," says Alexis, making the kind of joke Simone makes and liking how it tastes in her mouth.

* * *

Simone clicks into her terminal for Alexis's next first date, and when she sees who the date is with, she almost chokes. Alexis is on a date with Jason. Neurotic, goofy, charming Jason. It's not unheard of for pilots to encounter someone they know in real life while on the job. The Connect2 code of conduct doesn't forbid it; you just need to fill out an extra form disclosing your situation. Simone knows immediately she will not be truthful when she fills out the form about Jason. She has harbored what could only be referred to as a tragic crush on him for close to two years. Members of the same running club, they often fall into pace with each other, and have even grabbed breakfast together after their runs on occasion. Simone has hinted pretty aggressively that she is interested, but Jason, a paragon of tact, has never acknowledged her overtures. He's perfected his Friend Face—a look that says *I adore you, but nothing interests me less than seeing you naked.*

Simone as Alexis goes through the basic opening pleasantries with Jason, asking about his day and how he chose this place. She is always invested in getting a good outcome for her clients, but for the first time, she feels nervous. It's strange seeing Jason in date mode. His hair is still wet from a shower, and she's never seen this plaid shirt before. She feels a strange mixture of jealousy and titillation.

"There's this painting," Jason says. "I don't know the name of it or who painted it, but it's of this woman in a field, sort of looking over her shoulder at the painter or at someone. It's weird, but I keep thinking you look just like that woman in the painting."

"Where did you see the painting?" she asks.

"I had a postcard of it in my room growing up," Jason answers.

"I had postcards in my room, too!" She gets a quizzical burst from Alexis, who never collected postcards. Simone doesn't think including this one personal detail from her own life will blow the facade. She has never felt this tight, focused kind of energy from Jason before. There's no harm in enjoying it for a moment.

"I'm so afraid of rambling on and sucking all the oxygen out of the room," says Jason. "Tell me about yourself." Simone goes through her basic intro to Alexis spiel. Jason asks if she wants to stay for another cup of coffee. Simone does.

* * *

The next day, after a 5K, the whole running group goes out drinking. Simone and Jason are sharing a massive plate of nachos, the bar is playing one of Simone's favorite albums in its entirety, and life is good. Even though she knows she did not actually go on a date with Jason the day before, she feels closer to him. She shifts her weight under the table, rubbing her toe up the leg of Jason's jeans. He stands abruptly, saying the next round is on him. Their friend Diane approaches and starts talking about whether or not she should quit her job. Simone looks to the bar, catches Jason's eye, and he makes a face at her like *we know the same thing*. She knows it's not a great sign that when she flirts with him, he pulls away, but her gin and tonic is delicious, and she is invincible. Jason sits back down with Simone and Diane, and the three of them go over the few pros and numerous cons of her job.

"Simone, you like *your* job, right?" slurs Diane.

"Being a professional Cyrano?" teases Jason. "Who wouldn't like that? Simone gets paid to date."

"And I get glowing reviews," Simone preens. "Promoted three times in as many years, *and* my picture is on our recruiting pamphlet."

"The face of the faceless," Jason says.

"Let's play a game," says Simone. "Everyone think of a secret about the person to your left and whisper it to the person to your right." She leans close to Jason and whispers, "There's someone at this table I want to kiss more than Diane."

Jason smirks and bonks Simone on the top of her head. "Good secret, drunko." He leans over to Diane and whispers, loud enough for Simone to hear, "Simone has two levels, totally sober and totally wasted. Nothing in between."

Diane leans into Simone and whispers, "I fucking *hate* my job." She has not fully understood the assignment.

They stay out until closing, and Simone and Jason are the last two standing on the curb, waiting for their Ubers. Simone keeps reaching for Jason's hand, and he keeps holding it for a few seconds, then letting it go.

"I think you're just the cat's meow," says Simone. Then, taking his hand again, "I'm not tired yet."

"Simone. Not tonight," says Jason.

A minute or so later, his Uber shows up, and he gets in. Simone knows rejection when she hears it. But she can't help coming back to the possibilities that all non-tonight nights might still hold.

* * *

Simone is still feeling cocktails four through six from the night before when she meets Alexis for their next check-in. Alexis is paying three dollars a minute to meet with her, wrapped into her monthly bill, but Simone often gives her an extra ten minutes or so for free because Alexis is one of the sane ones. Simone genuinely would like to see a happy ending for her.

"For me, Jason is a pass," Alexis says, once they've briefly compared notes on the previous night's episode of *The Bachelor*. "He was so in his head. I felt like we were both so nervous; it was hard for me to get comfortable."

Simone is genuinely surprised. It's hard to picture someone not liking Jason. "To be fair," says Simone, "you don't usually feel comfortable when first meeting someone."

"I didn't take an official tally," Alexis says, "but I think he apologized to me, like, ten times over one coffee." Simone guffaws.

"Yeah, he did seem pretty eager to impress," says Simone. "If you want, next time I can keep an official 'I'm sorry' count from my terminal. We can make an over/under bet, and if you win, I'll let you give me a haircut."

"I think if I win, you should give *me* a haircut," says Alexis.

"You may find the results alarming, but yes, I'm in," says Simone, shaking Alexis's hand.

"So, you really think I should see him again?" asks Alexis.

"Has he reached out to you?" Simone asks, trying not to sound overly invested.

"He asked if I'm up for dinner on Friday," Alexis confirms.

"Tell him yes," says Simone.

* * *

Getting dressed for her second date with Jason, Alexis is thinking about soulmates. As part of the intake process at Connect2, clients have to describe how they picture their soulmate. Most people jot down a few sentences about being someone's priority or feeling sparks that mature into smoldering embers. Alexis wrote close to a thousand words. Alexis thinks a soulmate is someone who knows all of your thoughts and still accepts you. She thinks a soulmate gives you small doses of optimism when you can't get out of your own head. She thinks things that are hard for you will be easy for your soulmate. Where Alexis is shy, her soulmate will have chutzpah. Things that Alexis fears will be welcome challenges for her soulmate. Simone, trying to lighten the mood, proclaims all sorts of people and things to be her soulmate: the deli cat next door to Connect2's offices, the writer of that one SNL sketch that was actually really good, comfortable shoes, a nice breeze. The message, Alexis thinks, is that her soulmate might be right under her unusually sensitive nose. Alexis thinks Simone may be right about this.

* * *

When Simone clicks in for Alexis and Jason's dinner date, she sees that Alexis has not even worn one of her top ten date outfits, but Jason is looking sweaty and serious in a way that Simone finds lovely.

"I've got you," Simone says to Alexis, as she always does right before she flips the switch to take control. "This is going to be a good night."

* * *

Over dinner, Jason asks Alexis question after question. He asks if she can hear him chewing (she can), if she has ever gotten so mad she's wanted to hit someone (she hasn't), if she thinks David Lynch is going to make any more films (she doesn't care). As Simone's words come out of her mouth, though, Alexis realizes that Simone cares. She cares about David Lynch films; she teases Jason with a warmth Alexis doesn't feel. Alexis learns more about Simone on this date than in all of their debriefs together.

Alexis lets her mind wander, thinking about how strange being piloted is. She smells the flowers Jason has brought her, thinking *I am letting Simone smell flowers.* She raises her hand to her cheek. *Simone is touching my face. Simone tastes the sweet whipped cream I'm swallowing.* Simone has access to these thoughts, but is focused on the guy sitting across from Alexis.

The check comes, and Jason looks down. "So, I don't know if you'd want to, I dunno, go for a walk or maybe come to my place for a drink?" he says.

* * *

Simone has seen Alexis's engagement drifting as dinner has worn on, but she feels like she's on one of the best dates of her life. Especially when the conversation turns philosophical, and she can push aside Alexis's biographical specifics and share more of her own views. When she makes Jason laugh, she feels like a queen.

Simone doesn't see what harm a quick postprandial walk could do. She gets that Alexis isn't attracted to Jason, but she hasn't flipped the switch to take control and end the date.

"You live near here?" Simone asks as Alexis, knowing that he does.

"Just a couple blocks away." Jason smiles.

It has rained, leaving the air cool and the streets glistening. They cut across a park and, in a few minutes, arrive at Jason's building. Simone tries to soak in each second, knowing that Alexis will take control and end the date at any moment.

"God. I can't get over how beautiful you are," says Jason. Then he kisses her. It's a kiss Simone has been thinking about for over a year, and just the fact of it finally happening is mind-blowing. She kisses him back.

* * *

Alexis does not like kissing this loud-chewing, ever-apologizing guy. His lips feel gummy against hers. She's fascinated, though, by the idea that both she and Simone are in the same kiss. How strange, she thinks, to be a conduit for someone else's pleasure. Jason's hands are all over her now. His touches are all too gentle like he's trying to tickle her. Meanwhile, Simone is using Alexis's hands in ways she never would. She's pulling handfuls of Jason's hair, biting his lips. Alexis concentrates on being there but not there. She imagines herself as the spoke of a wheel, perfectly still, warmly wrapped in the embrace of perpetual motion.

* * *

Here are the things Simone most likes remembering from her night with Jason. The way that he put his hand between her head and the backboard of his bed so she wouldn't bang it against the wood. The fact that after taking off her blouse, Jason folded it and put it on his nightstand. Sure, it's not her blouse, not her head, but the experience was immersive. Her favorite memory is the few seconds of silence after they'd slept together, broken by Jason saying, with a goofy smile, "So, that was fun." Alexis hadn't flipped the switch until they'd finished coffee and a crossword the next morning.

She knows that if her supervisor digs into the logs for this date, it won't be good. Alexis's biodata didn't align with the choices Simone was making for her, and Simone has violated a clear rule against piloting a sexual encounter. Technically, it's a fireable offense, possibly even one with legal consequences. She's confident, though, that if Alexis really wanted to take back control, she would have. Maybe, Simone thinks, Alexis was even giving her some sort of gift—intuited Simone's investment in the moment and decided not to take it away from her. Simone knows she's done something wrong, but until an outside party tells her how wrong, she's going to assume the transgression was minor.

* * *

That Sunday, Simone sits across from Jason, digging into diner eggs after a run. Simone keeps trying to steal potatoes off Jason's plate, and Jason keeps pushing her fork away.

"What's up with you this morning?" Simone finally asks.

"It's nothing," says Jason. Then, after an uncharacteristic silence between them, "I kinda get the feeling that you don't love it when I talk about my romantic life."

"That's crazy. You can talk to me about anything."

"Okay. Well, I guess I'm in a funk because I went on what I thought was a really great date with this girl, but she ghosted me."

Simone fills her lungs with courage. "I mean, I know I'm not this amazing girl who ghosted you, but *I'd* be pretty into taking you on a date sometime." Jason looks at his eggs. Too many seconds pass. "Maybe a romantic trapeze lesson?" she appends lamely.

Finally, Jason arranges his features into Friend Face. "You're such a loon," he says, taking a forkful of potatoes and plopping them onto Simone's plate. "Eat your eggs and stop prying into my sad love life." Simone has been drunk on the great flood of serotonin coursing through her ever since the date. Here, in this overbright diner, rejected once again, she crashes hard. They finish breakfast in relative quiet, both thinking back to their own separate versions of the same night.

* * *

Alexis brings macaroons to her Monday session with Simone. For some reason, she wonders if Simone will bring some kind of confection herself—if they will be faced with an embarrassment of desserts—but when she arrives, Simone is empty-handed, slumped in her beanbag.

"So," Alexis begins, "crazy date, huh?"

Simone smiles weakly, then seems to resolve to engage and sits up a bit straighter. "I counted twelve on the apology tally, so I think I owe you a haircut," says Simone, but her eyes aren't fully smiling. The excitement Alexis had felt on the drive over starts to evaporate. It's not that she'd imagined passionately kissing Simone. She hadn't even imagined Simone thanking her. She'd just pictured the two of them sipping coffee and dissecting their shared experience.

"I don't think there's going to be a third date with Jason," she says carefully.

"Well, you can't force yourself to be into someone you're just not into," says Simone. Alexis wonders if Simone is referring to her own disdain for Alexis. She wonders if Simone thinks she is pathetic. To be rejected by someone who is literally paid to spend time with her would be a new low.

Meeting with Alexis usually energizes Simone, but today even Alexis's open face, her receptivity to all Simone has to offer, isn't enough. Simone knows what Alexis wants from her, abstractly at least. If she was piloting someone else in her shoes, she would give Alexis a hug, tell her the date had been wild and she'd never done anything like that before. Tell Alexis that she'd love to get dinner sometime, just the two of them. As both pilot and passenger, Simone can't get any of this out.

"What're all these boxes for?" Alexis asks.

"Well, my friend, it's the end of an era," says Simone. "Today is my last day at Connect2."

"Oh, did you...."

"My manager reviewed the logs from your date with Jason."

"Weren't you pilot of the month last month?"

Simone is briefly impressed with Alexis's memory. "Yeah, for the third time. But, they take the code of conduct seriously."

"I wasn't... I would have taken back control if... I mean, I think it was an interesting night for everyone." Alexis can't quite articulate why she let things go so far. It has something to do with the overfull sensation of being touched by one person while your thoughts stream to someone else. It has something to do with grasping for the only kind of connection you can reach.

"Being a star employee was sort of *my thing*," says Simone. "But, at the end of the day, I'm just a girl who gets fired for cause. Anyway, I guess they'll assign you a different pilot."

"I don't really want another pilot."

"Yeah," Simone sighs, with a roll of her eyes. "I'm basically irreplaceable." She takes a half-hearted bite of the macaroon Alexis brought. "These are good. You didn't have to do this."

"Oh, I know," says Alexis. "I wanted to." Then, reaching shyly into her bag, "I brought something else." Alexis pulls out a hairbrush and a simple pair of cutting scissors. She guides Simone from the beanbag to a proper chair, spreading an old sheet she brought from home on the floor around them. She smooths Simone's hair. She runs her fingers across Simone's scalp. She brushes out Simone's wild mane until it is a cloud around her head. She begins to cut.

"New do, new you, right?"

Simone feels herself relax, if only a little. She tries to breathe out Jason, breathe out her manager's disappointment, and breathe in the feeling of Alexis's hands at work. To embrace the idea that a macaroon and the friend who brings it to you is a thing of great value.

"This haircut is my soulmate," Simone says. She's not entirely wrong.

* * *

Discussion Questions

1. If you could have someone "pilot" you on a date, would you allow them to? At what point in the date would you want to take over control? After how many dates would you no longer want them to pilot you? Would you ever tell your partner you were piloted at the start of the relationship?

2. Is there a difference between being "piloted" by another person on a date and being the date version of yourself on a date? (*energetic, interested, funny...*) If so, what is the difference in presenting these two false versions of yourself?

3. Connect2 asks clients to describe how they picture their soulmate. How would you describe your soulmate? To be truly happy in a relationship, must a person date their imagined soulmate? Is a person settling for less if they date someone who doesn't exactly meet those ideals?

4. Given that Alexis could take back control at any time, did Simone do anything wrong by continuing the date through sexual intercourse?

5. If you could, like Simone and Alexis, share the experience and sensations of a sexual encounter with someone else, would you? Who would you share that experience with? Would you be obligated to tell your partner two minds inhabited the one body in front of them?

* * *

Room 101

J.B. Polk

* * *

Content Disclosure: Mild Violence

* * *

Winston must have been ten or eleven when John Smith, his father, told him, "You should read Orwell's *1984*. The protagonist has the same name as you."

Winston knew that he owed his name not to *that* Winston but to Churchill, whom John described as "the greatest statesman of all times."

"The lion who roared when Britain needed him the most." John was fond of clichés because, although he'd never set foot on British soil, he was a staunch supporter of the isle his ancestors had come from.

"I hope you grow up to be just like him—a stand-up man with strong values," John hammered into his son throughout childhood.

Winston was willing to oblige, but he soon realized he'd never be able to match Churchill's virtues, no matter how hard he tried. He preferred the other *Winston*, the one from the book, although he knew he was not a role model to follow.

He was weak. He betrayed the only person who truly cared about him. He cracked under pressure. Well, under torture, to be fair, but crack he did. Even before he was taken to the infamous Room 101 in the Ministry of Love, from where prisoners emerged broken, betraying principles such as loyalty, dignity, and integrity. And, like in Winston Smith's case, love. But it made him more human. More relatable. More flesh, bones, and blood. Less like the Winston his father adored.

Winston recognized that fear was necessary to keep people safe and cope with potential hazards even before he read the book. Many war heroes admitted to being frightened in extreme situations. Fear forced them to choose between the standard fight-or-flight scenarios. At the same time, fear, whether real or imagined, had the power to break a person, and Winston Smith's terror in Room 101 was not something he could fight or flee from; the only thing he could do was surrender and betray.

"What would my deepest fear be?" Winston wondered.

As much as he tried to think of something that would terrify him out of his wits, he couldn't come up with one single thing. True, he disliked spiders and heights, but not to the extent that would stop him from functioning. He didn't run from the room when he saw a creepy-crawly. And when he was sixteen, he climbed Mount Adams on a school trip and had a great time. Nothing could compare with his namesake's dread and his reaction to being told that caged rodents would destroy his face.

At first, Winston did not particularly like the novel. He read it out of a sense of obligation.

"You must read a book whose protagonist has the same name as you, right?" he told himself.

"To find the similarities and differences and, maybe, even learn from the mistakes. But that is as far as it goes."

For the next ten years or so, the book sat on a shelf in his room between *The Great Gatsby*, which he read for a school assignment, and *Harry Potter and the Philosopher's Stone*, which he read for pleasure several times.

But his interest was piqued again when, during the long summer before entering university, he had more time on his hands than he could fill. The novel drew him in. When he picked it up, he was met with the omnipresent Big Brother, who peered at people from four-meter-high billboards and trees, proclaiming, "Big Brother Is Watching You!"

It was more or less at the same time, but in a completely different context, that Winston came upon Big Brother's name in a TV program where a group of contestants, known as "housemates," inhabited a place called the BB House. The contestants spied on each other for financial gain and the chance to stay on the program under the watchful eye of ever-present cameras, much like the inhabitants of the novel's Oceania. Winston couldn't understand why somebody would deliberately lock himself up with fifteen other people to be live-fed twenty-four hours a day, doing things people generally did in privacy for millions of viewers to scrutinize. Those who were voted out were removed from the registers, and their one-time presence was forgotten, at least in the eyes of the audience, just as it was in the book. In other words, they were abolished, annihilated, and returned to the obscurity they had initially come from. It must have hurt a lot because they sought the spotlight and the attention of others.

The program was a hit, and the winners became instant celebrities who earned big bucks and their fans' adoration by exposing their most intimate secrets.

Apart from Big Brother, Winston specifically paid attention to the three slogans from the novel's opening chapter: *War is Peace, Ignorance is Strength, Freedom is Slavery.* The exact opposite of what he'd been taught by his parents, teachers, and leaders, including his father's idol. And what he usually accepted as the truth. Or, at least, A TRUTH.

"Perhaps," he said, "there's no such thing as one universal truth but rather something in between, equidistant from the slogans and from what has been hammered into us by years of formal education, Christian morality, and plain everyday living.

"Perhaps this is how society controls and manipulates our thoughts. How it realigns or reprograms our thinking. When we are taught that education is a strength, we believe it. But if our rulers change their minds and tell us that ignorance is positive, we will allow ourselves to be convinced that it is the only truth and nothing but the truth, so help us, God."

After reading the book for the second time, he again put it back on the shelf and out of his mind. At least until the moment that the dilemma of Room 101 came back to haunt him some years later.

Time passed, and Winston's life was far removed from the dystopian world of Orwell's protagonist. He graduated high school, dated, went to university, did a three-month internship in a local newspaper, and then realized that his degree would not land him a job to pay off his student loans. By age twenty-six, he was convinced that his education did not prepare him for real life. At least, not for a prosperous professional life permitting him to buy a thirdhand Chevy, rent a one-bedroom apartment in Missoula, and go on holiday in Hawai'i every second year. Not to mention daycare for kids, a wife's manicure, and weekly shopping at Costco. He had to find a job that would pay his bills and give him a sense of direction.

That was when fate led him to a neighborhood coffee shop, where while eating a crispy chicken sandwich with french fries, he noticed a banner quietly announcing, "Halliburton wants you. Provide the logistical backbone to US construction operations around the world."

Just like that. There was nothing about serving the homeland, appealing to patriotism, flags, or images of brave John Waynesque soldiers with pistols that would stir all kinds of internal fervors in a potential recruit. Just plain text with basic information and a phone number. Below, along a white-and-blue stripe, a list of exotic-sounding countries where the company operated: Somalia, Guyana, Nigeria, Serbia, Uzbekistan, and Afghanistan. Places Winston had only seen on maps, in NatGeo documentaries, and in holiday brochures he could only dream of visiting. Unless he joined Halliburton.

So he did. A few months later, dressed in a khaki uniform and steel-capped boots, equipped with a pump-action Remington 870 and a grenade-studded belt, he crawled into the belly of an EADS/Northrop Grumman KC-45 that would take him to Afghanistan.

Without realizing it, Winston was thrust into the sphere of influence of the first of the three slogans from the novel that had lain dormant in his memory: WAR IS PEACE from the beginning of his new adventure.

When the plane flew over Afghanistan, the guy whom Winston and the rest of the men only knew as Farrel said, "What you see down there are the Hindu Kush mountains. In Persian, Hindu Kush means Hindu Killer. You'll see a lot of killing once we land. Don't let anybody fool you into thinking this is a peace mission."

Winston's heart froze. Weren't they meant to provide the "logistical backbone" for the US construction teams? They'd been informed their task would be to ensure the safety of the new barracks, airstrips, and roadways. The recruiter didn't mention any killings. But if there were to be no killings, why had they been given such intimidating-looking weapons?

"For your protection," the Halliburton instructor had told them.

"You never know who'll be hiding in the bushes. Your role is to watch and inform. The army will do the rest."

"What rest?" Steve Dryden, a young buck-toothed farm boy from Alabama who'd joined at the same time as Winston, asked.

"None of your business," the instructor snapped.

"You do your thing, and the military will do theirs. You don't need to know, or rather, what you don't know won't hurt you!"

So even before leaving American territory, Winston had learned the meaning of the second slogan: IGNORANCE IS STRENGTH.

After a week, Winston discovered that things weren't that bad after all. There were no killings. The Halliburton team patrolled the fertile valleys, deep gorges, and high plateaus in amazingly rich auburns, caramels, and ambers mounted on enormous Humvees. They kept a close check on anything that moved and could endanger the convoys transporting construction materials and other supplies, reporting anything that could be noteworthy.

The work was not hard but quite intense on the mind. For eight hours, they focused on their surroundings, trying to spot potential sharpshooters or other sources of danger, such as Afghan peasants wearing grenade garlands hidden by their baggy shalwar kameez outfits.

"Avoid using your weapons or getting into any fracas with the locals. It's not your job," they were told, and they mostly obeyed.

In the evenings, they stayed in the camp, played cards and dominoes, read week-old newspapers and letters from their families (digital communications were restricted because the Taliban blew up transmitters near the headquarters), and talked just about anything. But most of all, they spoke about why they were there and what they'd do once they went back to Mancos, Colorado, where Bob Jensen was from, or to Fairhope, Dryden's hometown.

"When the military finishes their job here and frees the people from the Taliban, ah will get a quiet job driving a cart at the Grand Hotel Golf Resort. One hundred sixty acres of grass! Having driven a Humvee on the road full of bombs, ah think I deserve a break," Dryden sing-sang in his Alabama accent. He drew long and deep on his roll-up and released a perfect smoke circle.

"All ah'll have to do is avoid golf balls. Nice and easy. Because here, if ah drive over a cluster mine, there won't be enough of either you or me to send home. We'll all be blown to bits like confetti..." His voice trailed off as he stomped on the cigarette butt with the heel of his boot.

"Free the people?" Jackson Greenberg, a university student from the Midwest, laughed. Jackson had been kicked out shortly before graduating because of his radical views, which did not sit well with the university's conservative administration. Jobless and adrift, he joined Halliburton on a lark.

"You think we are here to free the people? You're off your rocker, man."

Dryden's face flushed with anger.

"Of course, we're here to free the people. Do you think they want to be ruled by the Taliban? Do you think they enjoy having their arms chopped off for stealing? Do you think Afghan women wear burkas because they think it's cool? That's why we're here! To free the Afghans and get rid of the Taliban!"

"You stupid Alabama country bumpkin! You've no idea what you're talking about!" Greenberg snorted, spittle flying from his mouth like miniature bullets.

"Don't they have newspapers in Fairhope? Or perhaps they don't teach you to read at all. We are here because the country has oil reserves and strategic minerals and because of the country's location. Afghanistan is a transit place for energy resources that the Taliban want to control. And so do we. And lots of other nations. But no one cares about the people! For all we care, they can keep being slaves, wear burkas, and have their hands and feet chopped off. That's how much we care!"

Winston realized at that point that FREEDOM WAS SLAVERY and that he came upon the third *1984* slogan.

The group's tour of duty was supposed to last six months, but they only had two weeks before being shipped back to the

Halliburton base in Houston for rest before being assigned to a new task. Their contract lasted an entire year, and Winston hoped to go somewhere more peaceful. Like Guyana, for example.

"There's no war there, and the job involves keeping a watch over oil pipe drilling, with plenty of nightlife, booze, and hookers," Carl Hamilton, who was on his third contract, explained.

In two weeks, Winston would be able to forget the windswept landscape of Afghanistan, where red dust snuck into every crack, and people were hostile and eyed them with resentment.

"Yes, Greenberg's right," Winston thought.

"We don't give a rat's ass about the Afghans, and they hate our guts. It'll be a relief to be somewhere I can talk to the locals without worrying that one of them will knife me in the back or torpedo me to the moon."

Two more weeks, and they'd be out of Charikar, where Haliburton was overseeing the construction of an airstrip.

"Out of the hellhole and back on US soil, God damn it."

It was probably one of their last missions, perhaps even the last one. They'd been ordered to survey the ditches around the construction site that carried no water but a trickle of crimson-colored mud. Plus, the building that once must have been a farmhouse but was now a heap of crumpled adobe bricks, contorted iron pipes, and red dust.

It was Winston's turn to take the frontline position. The remainder of the crew was lined up behind him in four rows of three individuals, four meters apart, in case they trod on a mine and were blown to the sky.

"Like confetti," Winston remembered Dryden saying.

He pushed forward, his Remington aimed at the structure, his feet shuffling in the bare earth, sending thick clouds of loose soil into the air. Even though the building was nothing but debris, a wooden gate with symbols whose meanings were known only to those who had left them there and who had most likely long since vanished swung from one remaining hinge.

"Perhaps they mean *war is peace*," Winston muttered, moving closer to the building, his chin shaking with unsuppressed nervousness.

It was a strange feeling to walk in the footsteps of so many lives now long gone and forgotten, not knowing what had become of those who'd spent their lives there, who'd painted the signs on the door, and who, most probably, were dead.

"Just this one mission, and I'll be out of the Killing Fields of Hindu Kush. One mission and a nice fat check will be yours, Winston Smith. And now, just focus because Big Brother might be watching you."

Behind him, he felt the others' movements. Four of his steps meant four steps forward for the team.

"Easy. Easy. There is no one there," he said in his head, although he sensed someone was watching him.

"It's a deserted farmhouse. Just that. There's no Big Brother."

He was now practically touching the door. With his outstretched arm, he pushed it. The hinge swayed and groaned open. Even though the roof had collapsed upon the splintered wooden rafters, it was still there, casting enough shadow to make it difficult to see inside.

Two more steps. One more. He was nearly inside now.

And then he saw her—a girl of no more than sixteen standing in a sunbeam. She wore a bright blue scarf around her neck, wrapping her face and covering her chin. What was once a pair of baggy pants was nothing more than pieces of fabric held together by a bulky belt. With one arm, she was clutching a child to her breast. In the other, she was holding something.

"Holy cow, it's not a belt," a voice inside his head said, but there was still no panic in his thoughts.

"It's a bomb, and she's holding the trigger."

She looked straight into his eyes. Hers were two green gems, strangely resembling the eyes of the lovely teenager National Geographic made famous in the eighties. There was the same defiance in her, the same look of determination, and Winston knew she was ready to press the trigger. He was aware that there was probably a circle of mines surrounding them and, if set off, they would destroy the ruins and the entire area around the house and the thirteen Halliburton men, including Winston.

Time stood still. They watched each other for what seemed like an eternity but could not have been more than seconds. Winston lifted his Remington and aimed it at the girl's forehead. She did not move, and the child in her arms was eerily quiet as if trained from an early age to keep silent under any circumstances.

At that moment, Winston understood where he was. He was in the Ministry of Love's Room 101, facing his worst fear: kill or die. Kill a teenager and a baby or die together with the rest of the men who relied on him. He had to decide quickly whether to become the Winston of the novel or the Winston with an unbreakable character his dad had wanted him to be. Press the trigger before she pressed the button in her hand. His life or hers... And the child's...

The anxiety was indescribable. He wanted to throw the rifle on the floor, cover his eyes, stop everything, and simply nurse his fear. But he knew he didn't have the time.

The image of a cage full of rats flashed through his mind. The image, however, was not the source of the terror. He dreaded having to work out in a split second what to do next. It paralyzed him. He tried to focus on every sensation in his body: the sweat that ran into the creases of his palms, the pulse that throbbed in his temple, the heart that beat so hard against his ribs that he could feel it directly beneath the skin. He concentrated on where the fear came from, thinking how much it hurt and how badly he wanted it to stop.

Time was running out. He had to decide. And he did...

* * *

Discussion Questions

1. What would be in your Room 101? Why do people have a unique Room 101 rather than a generalized one that applies to everyone?

2. If you were in Winston's position at the end of the story, would you shoot the girl holding the bomb and child? Why or why not? Do you think Winston pulled the trigger?

3. The story references famous slogans from Orwell's novel *1984*: "*War is Peace, Ignorance is Strength, Freedom is Slavery.*" Do similar slogans exist today? Are these slogans logical contradictions, or do they have a metaphorical meaning? Do you believe society can be manipulated to believe in slogans such as these? If so, how? If not, why not?

4. Winston says, "There's no such thing as one universal truth.... Perhaps this is how society controls and manipulates our thoughts. How it realigns or reprograms our thinking." Do you agree that there is no such thing as universal truth? Or is truth relative to what a society, culture, or individual believes? Is it easier to sway the opinions of those who believe truth is relative?

5. When Dryden from Alabama says, "Of course, we're here to free the people. Do you think they want to be ruled by the Taliban? Do you think they enjoy having their arms chopped off for stealing?" Do you believe he is imposing his own cultural values on others? Or do you think he is justified in believing no one would want to be ruled by violence?

* * *

The Compelled

Z.D. Dochterman

* * *

Content Disclosure: Existential Themes

* * *

"We want to rename the building 'The Ethereon Flux Parallel Worlds Center,'" the woman said. Lathar stepped toward her, having just taken the elevator up to the thirty-third floor. Slowly, her face came into focus: wide nose, a bob cut dyed green and purple, half-and-half, right down the middle. A small amount of blush applied to her cheeks. "So, what do you think of the name change?"

"I guess 'Transamerica Building' sounds a little small," Lathar said, "when you can send people to whole other realities."

She motioned him to the window, which opened onto the waters of the East Bay. Cars sped across I-80 toward homes in Emeryville, Fremont, and Hayward. All cities Lathar had helped build for the last three decades with townhomes and condos, cloud service centers and product warehouses.

With any luck, he'd be leaving that life in just a few weeks.

"Sorry, I didn't introduce myself," the woman said. "Hepnia Synol. Parallel Lives sales associate. You must be—"

"Lathar Jackson," he mumbled and extended his hand.

"Sorry, could you say it again?" Hepnia said.

He summoned what energy he had and added a bit more bass in his voice this time. "Lathar Jackson."

"Of course you are," she said and offered a glowing smile. "We've been anticipating your visit all week. You'll meet with Dr. Chen and the team in about thirty minutes." Hepnia invited him to sit on the brown leather sofa and took a seat opposite him. "In the meantime, we just have a little more intake, where I'll explain how the Parallel Lives LifeScan process works."

"Ask away, then." He interwove his fingers and clenched them tightly together.

"First let's start with how it works. As I'm sure you know, since Dr. Chen's discovery in 2034 of the existence of parallel worlds, we've realized that at every moment you make a choice, a new reality emerges, with a new 'you' and a whole new set of circumstances."

"Except my particles here are entangled with those of myself in every other universe. So at any moment, my quantum wave function is spread out across multiple parallel worlds." Lathar paused for a moment, and Hepnia raised an eyebrow, impressed. "Collapse the wave function, and this 'me' disappears and becomes another 'me.'"

"It seems we have a real expert. I'll just get through the standard stuff. Product description." Hepnia flipped through a few sheets of paper. "Here we go. For every branching choice you've ever made, there's often a better choice you could have made. And in several of the parallel worlds you're about to see in today's LifeScan, you made amazing choice after amazing choice."

"Unlike in this one, you mean," Lathar said with a gruff laugh.

"I don't know, Mr. Jackson. Trading subprime mortgages at twenty-three, founding Brambus by twenty-seven, and turning it into a twelve-billion-dollar real estate empire in less than two decades. Given the keys to practically every city from Richmond down to San Jose. Houses in Hawai'i, Malibu, Biarritz, among other places. I've read up on you, and I'd say you've made some excellent choices."

He leaned back and crossed his arms as his eyes drifted to the window again. *Excellent choices.* Eighty, eighty-five-hour work weeks. Too busy to even have kids with Eleanor. And then—at least that wasn't his doing—the accident. She was dead the minute the drunk plowed into her sedan. No time to say goodbye. At the funeral, he thought about how little time he'd truly given her over these last twenty-nine years. How little he really knew about her beyond a few petty details: born in Iowa City, had a taste for ravioli, sleeveless dresses. Loved to draw the intricate floral patterns on the tops of Corinthian columns and the faces of the Greek gods.

Everything after that was a blur. Lathar sold Brambus and moved to St. Lucia. Cocaine. Parties. Young women flown in from Miami. Before too long, fights started breaking out between the guys with too many drugs in their veins and too much money in their pockets. He'd wake up hungover, vomiting, and still somehow managed to gain thirty-five pounds at age sixty-two. It wasn't until the day that one of those women got shot, and Lathar had to hush it all up with the police that he decided enough was enough. Those were his excellent choices. Hepnia went over a few more details while Lathar nodded along as if in a trance.

"So Hepnia," he said during a lull in her questioning. "If you're in this reality, you must be living your best possible life, right?"

"Far from it," she said. "I'm saving up for a Silver-Tier LifeJump. I've heard you can even jump to a world that also has Ethereon Flux. So if you save up you can go Gold, Platinum, Diamond, all the way to—"

"Rapture-Tier. Just like me." Lathar looked around the room and settled on an old potted plant whose leaves had begun to wilt and turn yellow at the edges. "You done your Scan yet? See what other lives are out there?"

"No, but I'm so excited for you to do yours." Hepnia opened her desk drawer and pulled out a clipboard. "I just need you to take a look at this contract, make sure you agree to all the legal mumbo jumbo. Standard stuff."

"What's a normal number?"

"Of what?"

"Of different lives to see?"

"Rapture-Tier? We've only done three people at this point. But..." She leaned in close and began to whisper. "You know, I'm not supposed to reveal any of the details, but since they're not in this reality anymore..."

"Your secret will leave this reality with me."

"Fifty to seventy-five options was the range. I can't imagine! So many amazing lives you'll get to choose from." She handed him the clipboard, which had about five double-sided sheets of paper stapled in the corner. He started to sift through the document, looking for where to sign.

Ethereon Flux LLC enters into a binding agreement with client.... Advisory: may encounter violent or disturbing images during LifeScan Process.... Client must fill out final will and testament, will be considered legally dead in this reality.... Client may be temporarily detained for further testing should results reveal no parallel lives.... Ethereon Flux LLC does not make any claims as to the future quality of selected life.... All arbitration will be settled with Ethereon Flux (if existent) in secondary reality.... Not responsible for injury or death that may result from the LifeScan or LifeJump procedure.

Death was the last thing he was worried about. It was life, this life, that bothered him. He jotted down his initials on the empty lines and put his cursive signature with the date on the last page. Hepnia came over, took the documents, and tucked them under her arm. She picked up her phone, her eyes burning with excitement. Lathar scratched at the nail of his thumb with his index finger, then closed his eyes and felt how tired he was. Beyond tired, even though he'd done nothing for the last two-and-a-half years.

Just then, off to his right, the door swung open and three people emerged. Hepnia stood up and held out her hand, palm upturned. "Here's the team now."

Lathar immediately homed in on her, Dr. Chen. Eyes focused like a drill, taut mouth, with only the smallest wrinkles around the corner of her eyes. Shockingly good health for a woman of sixty-seven. Somehow, seeing her, Lathar thought Chen seemed smaller, more fragile, than the legend in the online magazines and newspapers. "Parallel Worlds Biggest Discovery Since Higgs Boson," one read. "Many-Worlds Interpretation of String Theory Confirmed Experimentally," said another. The easiest Nobel choice in history, they all agreed.

"Honored to meet you, Dr. Chen," Lathar said.

"The honor is mine," she said. "It's not every day we have someone who's transformed the landscape of our region as much as you."

"It's not every day I meet someone who's transformed landscapes throughout the multiverse," Lathar said and laughed. "I'm sure in one of those other worlds, I'm even more forthright about how impressed I am by you."

"In all of them, I'd tell you to save me the embarrassment," she said.

"Rick Ledgio, meager coder and binary cruncher of Dr. Chen's brainchild," the man to her left said, extending his palm. "My team built the LifeScan computers and machine you'll be using today."

"Long as your QA team is good," Lathar said. "Should be a painless ride, right?"

"The lives you'll see only get better from here," he said.

"And I'm Dr. Korver," the other man said. He had short brown hair and a thin layer of fuzz on his face that encircled a friendly smile. "I'll be here to ensure there are no negative impacts when your mind encounters all those parallel worlds."

"Hard for lots of people to deal with it emotionally, I've read," Lathar said. "Knowing there's a copy of them out there. Maybe robbing people at gunpoint. Or rotting in some cell, falsely accused of a crime."

"And how does having parallel lives feel to you?" Korver asked.

"Some people feel personal ownership over their

doubles," Lathar said. "Not me. I just want to find a better one and get there as fast as I can."

"Let's head to the room, and we can get you all set up with the machine," Chen said. "This way."

She swiped her keycard, and the door opened, leading them down a long hallway. Offices lined it to the left and right. Once they reached the far end, Chen swiped open another door and revealed a large room whose walls had a metallic blue luster. To Lathar, it felt like he'd been transported to a cross between a hospital and the interior of a spaceship. Four beds, each complete with an IV drip and a screen for vitals, lined the walls. Next to them, monitors flashed an array of cyan, magenta, and green. By following the cables, Lathar could see they were hooked into the large, boxy black computers below, each one about the size of a motorcycle. Two female and two male nurses hovered around in the background.

"Alright, Mr. Jackson," Chen said and motioned him to one of the beds. "It looks like we are all clear to get started."

Dr. Korver took out a metallic apparatus with electrodes and placed it on Lathar's head. Korver adjusted it and strapped it on snugly. "This device will send your brain into a superpositioned state. Basically, you'll be existing, mentally at least, in multiple realities at once. After—"

"Then," Ledgio said before Korver could continue, "it'll feed the computers information about your brain's electrical state, like its levels of happiness, as well as some of the factors contributing to it. Memories, friendships, material possessions. Our computer models will give us an assessment, with 99.99999 percent accuracy..." Ledgio double-checked each nine on his fingers to make sure he hadn't missed one. He nodded his head after reaching five and continued. "Basically, it will tell you what percentile life you are living among the billions of parallel lives you could be living at this moment on March 15, 2037."

"Remember," Korver said, "you will be the same age since we can't jump you into the past or future. But you may be able to jump into a world where you have a lower risk of cancer or, sorry, just looking at the chart here, lower blood pressure."

"Or maybe surrounded by people," Lathar said. "People I care about."

"Of course," Chen said. "That's what we're all about."

"Just one last question," Lathar said. "If other realities have invented LifeJump, how come we don't see people jumping into our reality?"

Ledgio took a step forward and clasped his coat lapel. "Most realities are somewhere near the 50th percentile. A simple bell curve, really. We're actually a little lower on the curve."

"Can't the LifeScan just find the world where everyone is living at their best? Imagine you've located it by now."

"Unfortunately," Ledgio said, "our computers seemed to have ruled out such a utopian scenario. For some people to enjoy their lives, other people must suffer. Peasants and nobles. Homeless men and millionaires. It appears to be a law of the universe as solid as entropy."

Korver called over the anesthesiologist, and the two of them began a long discussion. A television above Lathar's bed was playing videos of other LifeJumpers. Images of volcanic islands and deep black sand. Yachts and sunshine in tropical waters, coral reefs. Smiling faces. Some hiking to the top of mountains in the Pyrenees. Others relaxed with drinks on rooftops, overlooking the gossamer of city lights. But mostly, people were surrounded by loved ones. Wives, husbands, daughters, sons. Friends.

"Mr. Jackson, I'm Jiya," the anesthesiologist said. "Congratulations on your LifeScan. I'm going to help you relax first with this. How does that sound?"

"Perfect," he said. She inserted a syringe into his vein and pressed slowly. Jiya removed the needle and dabbed his arm with a square cloth.

"Now for the anesthesia. You ready?"

"So ready." Jiya found a vein in his left arm and put in the metal tip. He followed the tube with his eyes up to the IV drip. Now he just had to relax.

"As you drift off, you may begin to see a series of images." Jiya looked over at the screen to make sure his heart rate hadn't changed. "These will be the viewpoint of the 'you' in the alternate world. They usually go by extremely fast."

"Some people," Korver said, "compare it to seeing the whole universe in a second. Just try not to be too repulsed by anything bad or too drawn to whatever you find appealing."

"That said," Jiya said, "the anesthesia usually does its trick. It's extremely unlikely that you'll be aware of anything."

"Most importantly," Chen said, "when you wake up, do so slowly. Although you won't be aware of it, you'll have gone through billions, maybe trillions of lives. It's sometimes a little jarring to come back to this one."

Chen nodded at Korver, who drew closer to the bed. The psychologist reached in and flipped on a switch on the side of the electrode machine strapped to Lathar's head. The monitor above the computer started flashing with various lines. Erratic, upside-down V shapes. Although he wasn't exactly sure what they represented, he guessed they were brain waves or, perhaps, represented the contact his brain had already made with other worlds. After a few seconds, the monitor booted up a two-dimensional image of his brain, showing various areas lighting up and going dormant as time passed. The drowsiness had set in. It felt like he was floating on the waves in an ocean.

"Let's count backward from ten," Jiya said.

Ten. A memory came to him: a sun-dappled beach on Corfu. The turquoise water. Fine crystals of sand sifting through his fingers. Nine, eight. His wife, Eleanor. And then they were in the water, splashing each other, laughing like children, seven, and why didn't they take vacations like this when they were younger, I don't know he said, six, and she said why don't they start now, five, they had the money, it wasn't the money, it was just time, time, and he splashed her back, four, and smiled and said alright let's do it then, three, maybe I'll sell the company so we can do this, two, all the time, always. That was one of his last memories of her before the accident.

Before he could get to zero, Lathar had drifted off.

* * *

On waking up, Lathar noticed the room had dimmed considerably. His head swerved from side to side, and he tried to sit up but couldn't. A security guard stood about ten feet away, a rifle slung over his shoulder. One of the nurses, with the name tag Anthony, seemed to be taking notes, checking Lathar's vitals, then taking even more notes. The other nurses were shoulder to shoulder just a few feet in front of him, whispering to each other. Off to his left but further away, Dr. Chen looked to be wrapping up a phone conversation. Lathar's head felt heavy, wobbly.

"Welcome back," Dr. Chen said. "How are you feeling?"

"Little groggy, little cold," Lathar said. "Otherwise, good. Just felt like I slept. Like a dreamless sleep."

"Great," Chen said. She looked over toward the security guard and then back at Lathar. "Just don't move too quickly. Anesthesia can make you feel a little dizzy."

"Well, what can you tell me about my other lives?" Lathar said. "When do I get to see them?"

Dr. Korver pulled up a chair and sat next to him. He took a deep breath in and then exhaled, the warm air wafting across Lathar's arm. "I have some bad news. The computers haven't found any parallel lives for you."

"So your computers are messed up," Lathar said. "Run the scan again."

"We did," Chen said. "Three times while you were out. Each time, nothing. We decided to run it once more just now to be absolutely sure."

"I thought you said there were billions of lives, trillions," Lathar said. He sat up, and his face turned flush with anger. "I paid good money just so you could tell me—"

"It seems that all your parallel selves," Korver said, "have all already died in some way. And strangest of all, your current actions are not generating new quantum realities."

"Put simply, this is the only world that still contains *you*," Chen said.

"Then I'm no better than all the billions of people who can't even afford a LifeJump," Lathar said and put his forehead in his hands. "Stuck in their worthless lives." His voice had grown loud, and looks of concern spread over the nurses' faces.

At that moment, Lathar noticed Ledgio, who was on his cell, staring hard at him. The programmer seemed to be discussing something in a hushed tone. Jackson began to wriggle left and right and threw his legs over the edge of the bed. "This is ridiculous."

"I don't know how to tell you this," Dr. Chen said. Her voice, normally robust and confident, had cracked just a bit. "This may not be easy to accept, but we must keep you here for further testing."

"What are you talking about?" Lathar said.

"Under the Parallel Lives Act of 2035, the government has authorized us to keep in our custody anyone who has no parallel lives until their legal status becomes clear. For now, if you aren't actually generating new worlds when you make a choice, that means you're not really choosing between different possibilities. You're just doing what you are compelled to do in this one life. Like fate."

"But I want a different life," Lathar said and shook his hand in the air. "I must have free will because I want to be something else. Someone else."

"We will be detaining you starting immediately," Chen said and motioned the security guard to approach the bed.

"I didn't agree to that," he said. His insistence turned into a yell. "I did not agree to that!"

"It's part of the contract you signed," Dr. Korver said.

Lathar scanned the clauses in his mind. *Death or bodily injury. Legal will and testament.* Then, yes, he remembered having glanced at it ever so briefly: *Client may be temporarily detained for further testing should results reveal no parallel lives.* His face sunk, and a burning feeling welled up in his throat.

"So, what if I keep trying and can generate a parallel life?" Lathar said.

"We'd be more than happy to let you free," Chen replied. "Frankly, none of us want to keep you here against your..." She looked for the right word to finish the sentence but couldn't find one. "None of us."

"You won't have to," Lathar said and ripped the electrode machine off his head. Standing up, Lathar yanked the IV drips out of his arms and started walking toward the waiting room. The security guard cut him off and drew the rifle to his shoulder.

"Back in bed, Mr. Jackson," the guard said.

Lathar looked around the room and noticed a second guard at the exit. Anthony, Jiya, and one of the other nurses rushed over to him and grabbed him by the shoulders, arms, and midsection. As he struggled to get free, the three slammed his body against the wall. Dr. Korver walked over to grab something from the side table. Lathar flailed but could not unpin his arms from the grip of the nurses.

"This is criminal what you're doing," he said. "I want my lawyer."

"Of course," Chen said. "But for now, we need you to calm down."

Distracted by Chen's reply, Lathar failed to see Korver approaching from the right. The doctor had something in his hand. Something Lathar couldn't see. All of a sudden, he felt a sharp sting in his triceps. And Korver's needle was out before Lathar could even see it. Then the pain set in, and his arm began to swell. And then the drowsiness. The last thing he heard was the nurses' voices telling him everything would be alright.

* * *

When he woke up, Lathar could see that he was in a new room. Smaller, with dim lighting. Electrodes and the wiring that protruded from them ran across his chest, arms, legs. He'd been put in a hospital gown and was barefoot. One monitor showed a blue line plopping up and down as his heart shook with a steady, quick beat, while a second monitor tracked his EEG readings. He could see over his stomach and toes to the far wall where a security guard stood watch. Lathar reached up to touch his head, but he couldn't. His arms were strapped down to the bed. His scalp felt raw and itchy, probably having been shaved while he was out. A trickle of sweat ran into his eye. He blinked, over and over again, until the salty perspiration began to sting. Then tears tried to break forth. Not tears of sadness, just tears of exhaustion.

About an hour later, the nurse Anthony, came with a phone. "You wanted to contact someone?"

"Call this number," Lathar said and gave him the contact info of Elena Morales, his personal attorney. Anthony did as instructed and held the phone up to Jackson's ear.

"Elena, thank god," he said. "Chen and the psychopaths at Ethereon Flux are telling me I can't leave. I'm surprised they even let me make this call." He talked for the next ten minutes nonstop and explained all the details to her: the LifeScan, the lack of parallel lives, the 2035 law, the document he'd signed on entering.

"Don't worry about a thing," she said. "I'll file for habeas corpus as soon as we get off the phone. Contact your press people, and we'll put together a release. There's no way you can be kept against your will."

"That's just the thing," he said. "They say I don't have free will."

"If the judge denies habeas, it's the civil rights case of the century. The whole country will be on your side."

"In the meantime, I'm gonna just keep doing different things. Act weird. Do something unpredictable. If I generate a parallel life, they say they'll let me go."

"Seventy-two hours, you'll be out. Let's not even worry about anything else."

Lathar nodded to Anthony, who hung up the phone and put it away. Lathar asked the nurse for water, took a sip, and immediately spit it out on the floor. He moved his tongue in the shape of four-digit numbers. Snorted to the rhythm of pop songs he remembered from his youth. He looked over at the monitor. Nothing. No changes. Still no parallel lives. For the next three hours, no matter what he did, the monitor showed a black background with a flat green line. He was stuck.

About a week passed before the ruling came down. The judge had denied habeas corpus based on the Parallel Lives Act. Morales was shocked. Two weeks went by, then three. By that time, Lathar's story was international front-page news. Through Elena, Lathar heard that they were discovering more people without parallel lives and that they'd even come up with a new name for people like him, based on a term used in Chen's original research paper: *the compelled.*

About a month later, Morales began the trial of *Jackson vs. Ethereon Flux* in the San Francisco courthouse on McAllister, almost due west of where Lathar was being held. The idea of "temporary detainment" was being unlawfully applied, she argued. It constituted a form of illegal imprisonment when, in fact, Jackson had done nothing wrong. The judge, she claimed, should authorize his immediate release as unwarranted months-long detention was unconstitutional. The defense claimed that the Parallel Lives Act gave the government broad authority to hold anyone who had proved to be one of the compelled. By virtue of their lack of free will, now scientifically certified, the compelled had the same legal status as a robot, an animal. They could kill or steal and claim they had no choice and shouldn't be held responsible. The compelled were dangers to public safety. Ethereon Flux had to keep Jackson in its custody until the government determined what to do.

The judge sided with the defense, and, in a shock to both Lathar and Elena, so did the public. Anti-compelled activists seized on Elena's point that anyone could be one of the compelled. Quickly, the theory spread that crime came from those with no free will, no parallel lives, since good people would always choose something other than violence and harm. Some said Chen had proved criminals and the compelled were one and the same in her testimony. Local groups began to demand government testing for all to figure out who had free will and who didn't. In response, Congress boosted subsidies for Ethereon Flux to reduce the costs of LifeScans and set up local testing centers. People who didn't get tested were arrested in their homes.

In late 2038, Jackson's case went up to the Supreme Court. Along with the prior arguments, Morales argued that Chen's discovery should not create second-class citizens. The prosecutor showed that it was Lathar's decision to check for his parallel lives that led to his detainment, which constituted a sort of involuntary self-incrimination. On the day the ruling was set to come down, protestors had gathered in D.C. For every person demanding Lathar's freedom, there were five, six, claiming that the compelled represented a risk to national security. Minor skirmishes broke out throughout the afternoon, but the police finally separated the two sides.

At 4:22 p.m. on November 17, in a 5-4 decision, the Court ruled that Lathar could be detained so long as he showed no signs of generating new lives. Meanwhile, in his cell, Lathar had begun inventing new stories about alien races made of plasma who floated across space, decomposing and recomposing as needed. He babbled to the nurses about an underground pathway leading from the island of Corfu to the center of the earth in which a library with all knowledge was hidden in molten iron hieroglyphics. He told the guards about how the universe was a single conscious entity, playing itself out in atoms, light, gravity, and magnetic fields.

When she went to visit shortly after the ruling, Morales initially thought Lathar was trying to say increasingly strange things to prove he had free will, to generate a parallel life. But the more bizarre his rantings became, the more she saw he had come to believe them. By the end of the year, Elena was convinced that Lathar no longer understood why he was being detained or why he had begun to tell such strange stories. Morales asked a judge to transfer him to a psychiatric ward just before New Year's, but her motion was denied.

In March of 2039, the testing had concluded. In Phoenix and Atlanta, Detroit and Philadelphia, and dozens of other cities, the compelled were arrested and imprisoned: 4,275,382 in total. Out of that giant number, there were only two other millionaires, like Lathar. Steven Mycanos fled for Ecuador when someone inside the government informed him that he'd be rounded up. Jeremy Monroe, another real estate mogul based out of Wyoming, had managed to convince the government to just keep him under house arrest. Most of the others were held in temporary processing centers. There were fentanyl addicts, young and broke climate change activists, catalytic converter thieves. And there were immigrants from Guatemala and Honduras, men with nightshifts at the big box stores, and women who filled out shipping labels for the product warehouses. They were the ones who, so the computers said, had no free will, who were a threat to public safety.

The next month, the news came that Lathar, the first of the compelled, had died in San Francisco, in the building that had been renamed "The Ethereon Flux Parallel Worlds Center." The *San Francisco Chronicle* also noted one interesting fact. The security guard who was with Lathar at the time of his death heard him whispering a string of words that seemingly made no sense: "beaches," "gods," "Corfu," "work," "regret," "splash," "sand," "waves," "new life." But he was certain about the meaning of Lathar's final word, "Eleanor." It was the name of his wife.

When the doctors went in to pronounce him dead and haul the body away, they found something interesting on the monitor. At the moment of his death, Lathar had managed to generate some new lives in other dimensions. Lives where he did not die. Lives where he could show the guards the screen. Fetch Dr. Chen. Make his appeal that he was no longer one of the compelled.

In those other worlds, it would seem, Ethereon Flux would have to let him go free. In this world, they had made the right choice.

* * *

Discussion Questions

1. Assuming you did a LifeScan that showed you were not creating parallel universes and, ostensibly, were not exercising choice, would that cause you to conclude you did not have free will? Would it change anything about how you live your life?

2. If a person without free will/choice commits a crime, can they be punished for their crime? Do we punish people for their choices or their actions? Is there a difference?

3. If you could take a LifeScan and briefly see millions of parallel examples of your life, would you want to? What effect do you think seeing all those parallel examples would have on you?

4. If you would review and rate millions of variations of your life, by what criteria would you score the various lives as better or worse? (*financial, spiritual, friends, family relationships, etc.*)

5. What do you consider to be the two or three biggest choices you have made in your life that have directed your life toward being better or worse? How many of life's outcomes are simply random and not choice-driven at all?

* * *

The Lives and Time of David Hackman

Patrick Hueller

* * *

<u>**Content Disclosure**</u>: Intense Fight Scenes; Mild Language; Death or Bereavement

* * *

Remember David Hackman?

That's how we like to start: Remember that crazy son of a bitch?

The question is rhetorical for those of us who went to Stoneybrook Elementary. *Of course* we remember him. We talk about him every chance we get. At parties, at bars—anywhere enough of us have gathered.

Two or three of us doesn't cut it. We need numbers. And we need the uninitiated:

David who? they'll hopefully ask.

Where to start, we'll say, even though we know exactly where to start.

The first thing you need to know about David Hackman, we'll say, is that he was a spaz.

We don't mean that in a bad way, we'll say.

Not at all, we'll say.

It's just a statement of fact. David Hackman was a total fucking spaz.

That's why he went to the Spaz Box.

The *what?* one of the uninitiated will hopefully say.

The Spaz Box, we'll say.

We'll play it straight for a few seconds, wait for one of them to ask, What's a Spaz Box?

A box for spazzes, we'll say. Duh.

A *room* for spazzes, we'll amend.

Finally, we'll break: We know how that sounds *now*. But back then it didn't seem weird or harsh at all. It sounded logical. We had a handful of spazzes in our school, kids who had a tendency to have conniptions.

—meltdowns—

—tizzy fits—

—kids who would lose their shit at a moment's notice—

—every elementary school has these kids, right? —

—we called them *spazzes*—

—and when they did that—

—when they spazzed the fuck out—

(This is how we tell the story—all of us talking—our voices bleeding into one cumulative narrative.)

They got sent to the Spaz Box, which was just a room where this counselor

—What was his name again, Patrick?—

Chris?

(I'll say it like it's a question—even though I know that was his name. I don't want this story to be mine; I want it to be ours.)

—Right, Chris. Chrissy—

—That was David's name for him: Pissy Chrissy—

—Pissy Chrissy and the Spaz Box. We really were little animals, weren't we?—

Yeah, but it wasn't just us. Everyone talked like that. Even the teachers.

—It's true—

—No way—

Okay, so they probably didn't actually call it that. I mean, they couldn't have, right? But I honestly don't remember what else it was called—

—Neither do I—

—Nope. Me neither—

In my memory, Ms. Tollackson would say, "Dave, go to the Spaz Box."

—And he *would*—

—Just like that—

He'd be chasing someone with a glue bottle around and around the room, but when Ms. Tollackson gave him the Spaz Box order, he'd stop on a dime and say, "Wonder what Mister Pisster's up to."

—He didn't even need a chaperone or anyone to check on him—

—Except for the day Chris wasn't there—

That was the day Dave climbed into the ventilation system.

(We'll wait here for the inevitable reaction: *Really?*)

Really, we'll say.

—I don't know how he did it—

—Maybe he used a coin or something to unscrew the vent cover—

However he got in there, he wriggled his way up the vent.

—*Wriggled.* That's perfect, Patrick. He didn't just crawl. He fucking wriggled—

—No he didn't. Come on. You all keep saying that, but he didn't actually climb into the vent; he just talked into it from Chris's vent, through the wall, and out the vent facing the hallway—

—Screw you, man. He absolutely did climb into the vent. Jesus. We're trying to sprinkle a little pixie dust here, and you're fact-checking the best parts—

—Fine. I take it back. He wormed his way into the vent and pressed his face to the slats on the other side. Happy?—

—Ecstatic. So there Dave is, in the vent as *we all agree he was*—

—He was skinny enough to do it, that's for sure—

—Dave? Dave was a lot of things, but skinny wasn't one of them. That dude rippled—

—Not skinny *scrawny.* I mean skinny lean—

—Didn't have an ounce of fat on him—

When he got to the other side of the wall, where the other vent was, he was about head high.

—That's when he started talking to students as they walked by—

—"I am your conscience"—

—That's what he said!—

—All whispery and deep, but loud too—

—"I am your conscience. Give Dave Hackman all your

candy"—

—So fucking funny—

—"Give me, I mean Dave, all your Combos"—

—Remember Combos? I liked the pizza and pretzel ones—

(We can go on and on like this. Combos, Corn Nuts, Now & Laters. I honestly don't remember if Dave said all these things, but they're a fun blast from the past. And that's the point of this story: crazy, charming, nostalgic antics from yesteryear. If I remember right, and I do, David also said weird fourth-grade gutter-minded stuff: stuff like "Clean your crotch. It smells like farts." This was Dave trying to be shocking, to go way past what any other nine-year-old would dare say or even think, and it worked: Even now, as adults, we never repeat his most vulgar outbursts because they make our audience and us uncomfortable. That isn't the Dave we're trying to depict.)

Come to think of it, it was amazing we could understand a word that came out of Dave's mouth.

—What are you talking about?—

One of his teeth.

—Oh, right—his *tooth*—

—God, remember that thing?—

It was fake.

—Had a fake gum and everything—

—He could make it, like, suction to his real gum—

—But he never did—

All day long he'd swirl it around his mouth.

—Like his *tooth* was a Tic Tac or something—

—It's a wonder he didn't swallow it—

One time he shot it at another student.

—That crazy son of a bitch. He *blowdarted* his fucking tooth—

Dave rolled up a piece of construction paper and, when the teacher wasn't looking, shot his fake tooth at an unsuspecting student. One second the student was taking a test; the next he had a porcelain pearly white embedded in his cheek.

—*Porcelain pearly white*? Who the fuck talks like that?—

—Mr. Writer over here—

Who was the student again? The one who got shot?

(Of course, I know exactly who it was. But I don't want this to become about me. It's about us—all of us working together to remember the same Dave Hackman. It's the reason I mention Dave squirting glue on people but not the time he wielded scissors. Shooting a tooth might technically be violent, but it's idiosyncratic enough to also be charming. Scissors? That's too crassly aggressive to fit our image.)

—Jeremy—

—Williams? The dude who always wore the polo shirts and khakis?—

—Yeah, Jeremy the Jehovah—

—That kid was actually a surprisingly good athlete, but his parents wouldn't let him play sports or go to sleepovers—

The tooth got him right below the cheekbone if I remember right.

—Left a welt—

—I wonder how Dave lost the tooth in the first place—

—Was it always missing? It seems like it was always missing—

—I can't remember a time when he wasn't swirling it in

his mouth—

(I never interject here, even though I know the answer: no, Dave wasn't always missing one of his front teeth. I'm almost positive he lost the tooth sometime the summer before fourth grade, and I'm equally sure I know how. Unlike the others, I went to Dave's place once—which is something else I've never admitted out loud. I'd rather think of Dave in the same way everyone else does: an odd acquaintance at best, his inaccessibility making him easier to mythologize.)

* * *

Our friendship was brief. It began and ended over the course of a few days during the summer after third grade. It was an alliance of shared geography, I think, more than anything. Third graders are still young enough to have those. I was new, not only to the apartment building but to the town. At nine years old, I didn't understand a lot of the reasons for the move, mostly because I didn't want to, but I did understand that my mom had lost her job at 3M and that Dad didn't make enough—he taught middle school English—for us to live in our house anymore. Most importantly, I understood that this was temporary; that's what my parents told me over and over, and that's what I told myself when I wasn't busy trying not to think about the situation at all.

To say that I had a plan for getting through the summer would suggest that I'd taken the time to devise one—I hadn't— but I did have a coping mechanism: reading. The only boxes I bothered to open that summer were the ones labeled *BOOKS*. I read all the Roald Dahl and *Goosebumps* and Matt Christopher books I had. When I'd finished them, I moved on to my dad's teaching boxes. *The Outsiders*, *Tom Sawyer*, *Lord of the Flies*—the usual middle school stuff. Looking back, it's amazing that I never read *A Separate Peace*. Not that summer; not at all until a few years ago. Did my dad not teach the book? Didn't every middle school English teacher used to teach that book? All my classmates seem to have read it. They brought it up once, at some reunion, when they asked what I wrote about, and I reluctantly admitted I mostly wrote literary fiction. "Stories about regular people doing regular things," I quickly added. Note: why do we have to call it that? *Literary* fiction. Maybe it's my Midwestern-ness, but calling what I do *literary* makes me feel like a pretentious putz. "You mean like English-y books?" one of them asked. "Like, did he or didn't he push the other kid off the branch? We must have had to talk about that for like a month." When I admitted I didn't know what he meant, Jerry polled the others: "What was that book where...?" How I'd missed *A Separate Peace* when everyone else seemed to have read it, they weren't sure—or very interested in figuring out. Their enthusiasm faded the moment they landed on the name of the book. I couldn't help wondering, though—after I *did* read the book—if I'd somehow managed to block the entire experience. Especially the scene in the tree. *I'm not sure*, I should have told Jerry. Do I spend my time writing (and teaching) stories like *A Separate Peace*—or do I spend my time trying to avoid them?

But I'm getting ahead of myself...

The apartment: Sometimes my parents would insist that I go outside—"You can't just spend the summer cooped up in here, Patrick"—and I'd walk down the hallway, a book tucked away in the waistband of my shorts, take a right, and, still very much inside the building, sit down with my back to the wall. I rationalized that I wasn't disobeying my parents' order, at least not directly: after all, they told me to get out of our apartment, not the entire building. What is it with kids' affinity for technicalities? In my case, I think it had to do with reality; that is, with my desire to avoid my own reality by reading about others. This was not pure escapism, I don't think; I wasn't pretending to be Tom Sawyer. It was a distraction. In retrospect, I'm not exactly sure why moving to that apartment was so scary; it's not as if we ever missed a meal. Perhaps it was *because* I didn't ask questions or even acknowledge my fear that it grew so out of proportion. I allowed stories and characters to clutter my concerns about lack of money and of friends. Paradoxically, by staying inside the building and hardly moving, I thought my current situation would feel less paralyzing; if I went outside, I'd have to face the building and my reality head-on.

I think that's how David and I met. I had my head in a book, and I happened to be sitting near his apartment door. I say *I think* because it's possible my memory is playing tricks. By attributing cause and effect, we remember childhood moments as if they were more, well, momentous than they seemed at the time. Even that phrase, *meeting people*, is too adult. Kids don't meet; they hang out. I'm pretty sure Dave didn't even bother saying hi or introducing himself.

Instead, he asked two questions.

The first being: "Did anyone go in this apartment?"

I must have looked up then. I must have seen Dave standing over me. He was probably shirtless because, weather permitting, he had his shirt off whenever he could, even at school. He would have already had that preternatural six-pack, those tight-skinned pectorals. He would have also had the scabs and bruises that seemed permanent fixtures on his body—

injuries that went unquestioned, at least by other kids and I think by teachers too, because of Dave's wildness. He must have gotten them, everyone instinctively reasoned, climbing trees or fighting feral cats or doing God knows what.

He must have also been literally twitching with energy that day in the apartment, just as he twitched with energy every day that year at school.

"What?" I asked.

"Did anyone go in here?" he repeated.

I think my answer was non-committal; I hadn't seen anyone, but then again, I hadn't been looking. To this day I can get so engrossed in what I'm reading that I tune out my surroundings.

David turned the knob carefully, as if he didn't want to disturb anyone. He peered into the apartment, then smiled at me with what I'm almost positive was a full set of teeth.

"I didn't think so," he said. Then he asked his second question. "Wanna play Nintendo?"

Why did I agree? Was I hoping to make a new friend? Was his twitching making me nervous? Dave had a way of getting kids and even adults to do things, I later learned, by making them nervous. In gym class he'd change teams whenever he wanted, and no one would object, not even the teacher. It was just easier to go along with his whims than risk him going ballistic or running away or, I don't know, tearing off his clothes and streaking across the field. (Yes, he did that once.)

Then again, maybe I accepted Dave's Nintendo invite as a vicarious way of gaining re-entrance into the apartment I'd recently been kicked out of, or, for that matter, the house I'd almost as recently been removed from. We *had* sold our

Nintendo a few months prior to help with a mortgage payment, so maybe psychology really can offer some insight—but I doubt it. I think I went into the apartment because I went into the apartment. No cause, no effect.

In Dave's apartment, I took a few turns at first, but soon enough he was playing for both of us, and that was fine by me. He played and I read. The apartment was cooler than the hallway, and I didn't have to worry about my parents catching me and confiscating my book. I also didn't have to worry about paying attention to the clock. Right around dinner time, like clockwork, Dave turned off the video game and told me we'd better go. I didn't ask *Where?* because I already knew—anyway, I knew where I had to go: back to my apartment. If I wondered back then why he was leaving his home right when every other kid was likely going to theirs, I didn't ask. I was too busy coming up with a reason for why I hadn't tanned or burned despite supposedly playing outside for much of the afternoon.

I don't know how many days Dave and I hung out. Three? Four? Enough that it became a ritual. Enough that it felt like a comfortable, predictable part of my day. Enough that I stopped noticing Dave's twitching, or the way he kept his head on a swivel as he played. Enough that I felt more or less relaxed in this foreign apartment, and maybe he did too: maybe I stopped noticing the head-swiveling because he stopped doing it so much.

Did he lose track of time, or did his brother arrive early?

Either way, what happened next happened next quickly.

A door banged open and slammed shut; a hand smashed into the back of Dave's buzzed head. His body lurched forward toward the TV, and his brother—although of course I couldn't have known who he was back then—grabbed him by the ankle and dragged him, skin screeching, across the peeling, wooden floor.

"Fucker," the brother spat out.

For years afterward, I remembered Evan saying something like, "How many times do I have to tell you not to play my Nintendo?" But I'm starting to believe that this memory is false. After all, if he *did* say this, it would have been the longest sentence he uttered, as well as the cleanest. I think it's more likely that I added this information just as I added the knowledge of Evan's name and relation to Dave. I needed him to say that Dave had broken some rule, needed him to give some reason for his violence. The alternative—entirely spontaneous and vicious cruelty—was too horrifying to consider.

Whether or not Evan asked the question, Dave didn't answer. His body was curled and fetal, and all he could manage were whimpers.

Later, I learned that Evan was only three years older than us, but at the time he might as well have been in his twenties. I don't know where he'd been during the day, but his muscle shirt was yellowed and drenched with sweat. He had the same musculature as Dave but more bulk and more hair covering it. I want to say that I remember his sour sweat smell, like huffing a damp, dirty towel, but my memory's probably reaching for sensory specificity that didn't occur to me then.

"Stop it," I said. *I said that.* I'm sure of it. It was just the once, and I doubt it was loud, but it got Evan's attention. For maybe the only time in my life, up until then and definitely since, I spoke up on another's behalf.

"Fucking... who the... fuck..." The words came heaving out

of his mouth as he lunged his body into the air and headed my way. "Hey, fuckface," he said over his shoulder. "Who the fuck is this?"

He stood towering over me, hands clenched.

"Fuck you."

It wasn't me who said this. I was done speaking up.

It was Dave.

I'm not sure that, in my horror, I comprehended much of what I saw next. But in retrospect, I (mis?)remember seeing Dave manage to sit up. I (mis?)remember him rubbing the back of his buzzed head, looking at his blood-covered hand. I definitely remember him once again mumbling, "Fuck you."

Then saying it louder: "Fuck. You."

Then continuing to tell his brother to fuck off until Evan turned away from me and resumed beating the shit out of Dave.

Lastly, I remember Dave telling me to get the fuck out of there, and, dear God, I hope that part of the memory is accurate. I want so badly to believe that Dave gave me permission to leave, preferably with no expectations or strings attached.

Because I *did* leave.

And I never returned.

As an adult, I've built a solid self-rationalizing architecture around this desertion. I've told myself that I was only a kid, and I was terrified, and, again, *I was only a kid* (because that point above all exonerates me, right?). In low moments, I've iterated and reiterated to myself that Dave wasn't trying to save me, that he probably had his own reasons for directing his brother's wrath back his way. I've generously bestowed upon my childhood self an obtuseness that I likely didn't possess: I was an only child, I tell myself; maybe I thought I was witnessing normal older brother behavior?

What's undeniable, whatever my reasons for not reporting the incident to my parents, is that I continued to operate as though I didn't have to face bad things if I didn't want to. This avoidance turned out to be as simple as taking a left down the hallway instead of a right. Within a month my mom had a new job and we had a new house.

What was harder to avoid as I got older was cause and effect.

I've expended considerable creative energy trying not to think about what caused the scabs and bruises on Dave's body. Or why Dave needed to get a fake tooth. Or how much responsibility I should take for everything that happened after that day in the apartment.

None, preferably. If I could choose—and for most of my life I've acted as though I could—I'd take no responsibility whatsoever.

* * *

—Remember Cube City?—

(It's at this point that I let the rest of the group take over completely. I may be the one who always brings up Dave in the first place, but once I do, they never fail to reference Cube City.)

—Right in the middle of the school library—

—A magical mystery palace—

—A super-duper structure... thing—

—Imagine a bunch of blocks stacked on top of each other—

—It was for reading. We were supposed to climb up the blocks—

—While holding a book, I guess—

—Right. We were supposed to climb up the blocks *one-handed*—

—Okay. So maybe it wasn't that well thought out—

—Did we mention our school was weird?—

—During recess, we could go outside and play *or* go to Cube City and read—

—You know what would make this jungle gym even better? A fucking book!—

—What kid in their right mind would choose reading over playing?—

—Willow Swenson, that's who—

—I said what kid "in their right mind"—

—Big, bowl-cutted Willow Swenson—

—She was perched all the way at the top of Cube City—

—I don't know how she managed to get herself up there—

—Personally, I think she fell during the climb—

—That's not what she said. Remember? The assembly?—

—She said she was reading and she must've forgotten where she was—

—Just leaned back for a wall that wasn't there and—

—SPLAT—

—Knocked out. A broken arm—

—And who comes to the rescue?—

—David Effing Hackman—

—Why he was there, I don't know—

—Was that kid *ever* anywhere you expected him to be?—

—Anyway, he picks her up and runs her to the nurse's—

—This was not a light girl—

—This was a hefty girl—

—This was a fat girl. What? The girl was obese—

—David picked her up like it was nothing—

—We know because he did it again at the assembly the next day—

—She told her story and then, whoop, with no warning, Dave lifted her off the ground and cradled her like a baby—

—Got a standing ovation and everything—

—I can still see him grinning that missing-tooth grin—

* * *

Depending on alcoholic intake, they'll stand up right there and then and clap for the memory of Dave at the assembly. Sometimes our audience does too. But I can't join them. Because as much as I want this to be the real story, the *complete* story, it isn't. I keep thinking that I can make it the whole story through repetition. But the opposite happens. It's Hemingway's iceberg theory: all that ice below the surface. Most of my creative writing students misunderstand Hemingway's writing as empty. And yes, I still teach Hemingway. I know he's been written off as datedly, pitifully, irredeemably macho and humorless, but the man found powerful ways to say things without saying them, no matter how easily dismissed his books have become. At best, my students seem to think, to write like Hemingway means to write short sentences that reveal little to no background info or physical description. But that doesn't do him justice. For one thing, he often wrote long, elegant sentences; check out his writing on bullfighting, if you can stomach such brutality. More importantly, Hemingway wasn't interested in what he called "hollow places," total absences of meaning or information; he was interested in omission. The key was that the reader was aware of the omission. That distinction between hollowness and omission isn't just semantics. It has major dramatic repercussions. It's the difference between seeing a guy with a mysterious fake tooth and knowing how he got it.

The Cube City story is commendable to others because they can't see what's being omitted, or even that something *has* been omitted.

I can.

Because I was there.

And I therefore know that Dave did more than come to the rescue. He caused the fall in the first place.

Anyway, I think I know that.

Admittedly, my view was obstructed; I couldn't see exactly what happened.

Not exactly—but pretty much.

Cube City was indeed a "structure thing." More specifically, it was a series of three-dimensional wooden squares piled on top of each other. There were four squares per level, three levels total. The squares were open on two sides; that's where you entered. They had either a roof (first level), a floor (third level), or both (second level).

I was on the second level when Dave climbed by. There was a ladder, a series of planks, to help students get up and down, but Dave hadn't bothered with it. By the time I noticed him, all I could see were his legs. They dangled in front of me, his dirty light-up sneakers flickering as his toes bumped the side of my cube.

I don't know what I was thinking at that moment. Was I in that weird head space between reality and whatever book I was reading?

I do know what I saw: Dave's legs straining and kicking; Willow plummeting to the floor.

When did I realize it was Willow? I didn't catch more than a glimpse of her fall, and besides, I was still new at the school and struggling with names. At any rate, I definitely knew it was someone; otherwise, I doubt I would have scrambled to the edge of my cube, the one unobstructed by Dave's legs. There she was, lying in a heap on the carpeted floor. And then there *he* was, also falling but unlike Willow landing on his feet.

Like I said, I can't know for sure that Dave was directly involved in Willow's "accident." Perhaps she really did just lean back too far. Perhaps the whole thing was just a coincidence. As the others like to note, Dave was capable of showing up just about anywhere. It's possible, I suppose, that he just happened to be hanging from Cube City, from the box Willow was sitting in, and that his legs just happened to flex and jerk at the exact same moment that Willow teetered from her perch.

That's what I want to believe.

But the truth is, I don't.

I don't know why Dave would do something so spontaneously vicious, but then again, I don't know why he did any of the things we still talk about today.

I've come up with a theory, though.

Maybe Dave acted so arbitrarily violent for no other reason than, like his brother, he *could.*

No one could do a thing to stop him. Anyway, no one *would* do a thing to stop him.

By *no one*, I suppose I mean Willow. If she was pulled off Cube City, she never said so. Then again, she said she didn't remember much of anything in the moments before her concussion. And even before she fell, she was more than a little spacey.

By *no one*, of course, I really mean me.

Why else did Dave stand there for a few long seconds, cradling Willow and staring me down? Maybe he wanted me to know that *he* knew. Knew I was there; knew it didn't matter.

Knew that, once again, I wasn't going to do a damn thing to help the victim.

Am I being solipsistic? Am I, in my guilt, making something about me that isn't?

Possibly.

But that's the thing about adulthood. It's the thing about narrative. We can't help but impose cause and effect for the sake of a cohesive story.

The image I have of Dave holding himself up with one arm and yanking Willow down with the other is false only in that I couldn't have actually seen it. I didn't have the proper angle.

But like Hemingway's iceberg, I didn't need to see everything to know what was there.

Especially given what transpired the next summer.

* * *

—I wonder what happened to Dave—

—You *know* what happened to him—

—I mean after that—

(At some point, someone in the crowd will ask *After what?*)

—Dave's brother got killed—

—*Murdered*—

—By his old man—

—You might have heard about it. It was all over the papers—

(That's how I finally learned Dave's brother's name—in

the papers.)

—It was fucking grisly—

—Remember his dad—

—Dude was built like the Hulk—

—Beat his own kid unconscious and bloody—

—Let's not get into it. They get the gist—

—The gist is we never saw Dave again—

—I heard he went to live with his relatives out east—

—Or was it out west?—

—Somewhere far away—

(We're from the Midwest; everywhere that isn't right here feels far away.)

—Never saw that poor crazy bastard again—

* * *

I never saw him again, either. But I tried. I don't know for sure what compelled me to walk back to the apartment, but I think what jumpstarted me was the realization of our continued proximity. The house we lived in was only six blocks from the apartment, and in the days following Evan's murder, it occurred to me that Dave and I were still practically neighbors. Until then I'd convinced myself that I'd moved far away—it might as well have been the east or west coast—but the relentless sound of sirens on the night of the murder proved otherwise. I think I also felt the need for reassurance. I wanted to know Dave was okay. I wanted him to give me permission (there's that word again) for the relief I couldn't help feeling: this horrifying monster of a brother was gone, finally, from his life—and from my life too. Of course, once again I was being selfish, but I masked my selfishness with the excuse that I just wanted to check on Dave's well-being.

This was the summer after fourth grade; I'd turned ten only a few weeks prior. I was still young enough to act impulsively without anyone expecting much of an explanation. I could still get away with doing something just because I got the urge to do it.

I walked out of my cul-de-sac, out of my neighborhood, past the gas station across the street, past the nursing home to my right. Adrenaline's a funny thing: sometimes it speeds everything up, makes it blurry, makes it so events seem to be skipping ahead, almost as if you've blacked out. Other times, it slows everything down, makes it more vivid, makes the air itself seem fresher, clearer. I always tell my students that good stories take place in "real" time, that is, time as we experience it. I encourage them to modulate their narrative, their scenic descriptions, based on emotion rather than the second hand of a clock. The more adrenaline your characters feel, the more you should either speed up or slow down. That day, as I made my way to the apartment, I experienced the latter. I felt my heart beating in my chest. I felt every swallow and blink, almost as if they were decisions I was making. My bodily operations had apparently gone inside out. Blinking was under my purview, but walking? Walking was autonomic, mandatory. My feet worked independently of my brain. Several times I thought about stopping, reversing course, or merely stooping and scooping up one of the maple helicopter seeds that littered the grass. But I didn't do any of these things. I just kept going.

It was only three or four days after the murder, but I was somehow still surprised that so many cop cars were camped out in front of the apartment. Hadn't they solved the crime? The papers and the local news had already identified Dave's father as the primary, in fact the only, suspect. The cops had found him in the apartment, drunk and insensate and covered in blood. Did I know this information yet? I must've known some of it: my parents, assuming I was still asleep or at least in my bedroom, cranked up the volume of the TV news and of their own voices. *Can you believe what that man did? To his own child?* I guess I assumed that there was no reason for further investigation. My parents were adults, after all; if they knew so matter-of-factly what had happened, the whole adult world must have known too.

But there the cop cars were, as well as the cops themselves: sitting in their cars, some of them, others standing by the entryway.

I thought I'd be able to stroll right into the building as though... what? As though I still lived there, I guess.

No such luck.

The cop at the door told me I better turn around and get on home.

(I'd walked six blocks only to get turned away at the door.)

* * *

—Remember the last time we saw him?—

—You mean at the tennis courts?—

—It was only a couple days after school had ended—

—We were playing home run derby—

—The fences are nice and high on a tennis court—

—It's like you're hitting the ball over the green monster in Fenway—

—Dave shows up out of the blue—

—He wasn't invited—

—I didn't even know where he lived, did you?—

—No clue—

—Me neither—

—Dude just *appeared*—

—And he says, "Can I take a turn?"—

—Did he even say *Can I?* He might have just said, "My turn."—

—I think it was Lance Marsden who tried to hand him the bat—

—But he didn't take it—

—He took the ball—

—From the pitcher—

—I don't know if he thought we were playing an actual game or didn't care—

—What he wanted to do was pitch—

—*Really* pitch—

—We'd been throwing the ball half-speed so the hitter could easily hit it—

—Plus, it's not like the kid playing catcher had any gear on—

—But Dave starts hurling the baseball as hard as he can—

—And none of us had the cojones to stop him—

—Luckily, right then, Ms. Tollackson strolls by—

—And Dave sees her and runs to the fence—

—"Hey, Ms. Tollackson!"—

—He's screaming, but not to scare her—

—He's, like, overjoyed—

—"Hey, Ms. Tollackson! Ms. Tollackson! Have a great fucking summer!"—

—That's what he said—

—We're from a small town—

—Well, we're from a suburb that used to be a small town—

—This was the summer after *third* grade—

—But here's Dave yelling—

—Totally casual, like it's totally normal, like he means it in a positive way—

—"Have a great fucking summer, Ms. Tollackson!"—

—He just stood there screaming at her, banging the fence, trying to get her attention—

—At the time, it seemed so crazy—

—But now? Now it seems almost sweet—

—I guess he just wanted her to acknowledge him, answer back—

—"Have a great fucking summer as well, Dave."—

* * *

I can't remember Dave yelling at Ms. Tollackson because I wasn't there. I was still one lonely summer away from making enough friends to get invited to a home run derby.)

But I want to. Remember.

I want to have this memory for myself.

I want it to replace the other memories.

That Dave Hackman, the one who good-naturedly cussed at our teacher, is scary only in lovable ways. Students kept their distance, but they weren't truly afraid. If anything, that distance gave them a better narrative perspective from which to report his antics. Nor did you have to feel sorry for Dave. He never let on that he needed anyone else. If he *did*, he'd simply join their team or their game.

That Dave didn't bother asking for anything; he took it, usually with a twitchy smile on his face.

When people hear stories about this Dave, they shake their heads, amazed—but I think they relate too. At some primal level, I think they admire this Dave for doing and taking whatever he desired.

I want to believe that *that* Dave can exist on his own and forever independent; that there doesn't have to be a flipside, that the other Dave, the Dave I witnessed, the Dave I saw only briefly but then never stopped seeing, that *that* Dave is the false one, the figment of my imagination, a hollow space instead of an omission.

And maybe this isn't wishful thinking on my part. The facts are the facts. Willow fell and Dave carried her to the nurse's—that's a fact. Evan was killed and his father was found at the crime scene. That's another fact. It's also a fact, according to the newspaper articles I've read over and over, that the father offered no countertheory for what had happened. When cross-examined, he apparently didn't answer many questions. He just repeated, over and over, "I love my boy."

The question that I can't help asking, though, is: *which boy?*

When I arrived at the apartment three days after the murder, I waited my turn to get in. I watched the cop open the door for two elderly women, and I attempted to follow them inside.

"Whoa there, son," the cop said. "Who do you report to?"

At the time, I felt like he was interrogating me. But looking back, it's more likely he was doing that thing that adults sometimes do when talking to kids. It's odd, but adults seem to take some amusement (or reassurance?) out of asking kids questions they don't know how to answer. They seem to like to see kids squirm. My mother had a friend, for instance, who would never say her name when she called. This was before caller I.D. It was back when parents instructed kids to never divulge personal info over the phone. I'd ask who was calling, and my mother's friend would say, "Who's picking up?" We'd go back and forth like this. At six or seven years old, I experienced these exchanges as deeply unnerving, but she experienced them as gentle teasing.

Which, I suppose, is the point: adults don't see anything particularly sinister in unsettling children. By the time the cop clarified his question, he accompanied it with a smile.

"Do you live here?"

I told him I used to.

The smile became a frown. "Only current residents allowed, I'm afraid."

I don't think I was demoralized by these words. I might have even been elated. After all, I'd *tried* to be there for Dave. This time, finally, I'd done my best; clearly, there was nothing else I could do. I'd been let off the hook and could leave with a clear conscience.

Before I had a chance to turn around, the cop spoke up: "Did you know them? The boys?"

I don't think I answered him, but I might have nodded.

He told me he was sorry. Then he continued talking. I'm not sure why—for my benefit or his own? His speech kept halting, and I kept trying to leave, but then his voice would start up again. It was awkward. All those meaningful looks. Was I supposed to say something? What? He certainly didn't seem to have much substance to share—not at first, anyway. "A thing like that... horrible... I'm sorry... I'm really sorry, son." Maybe he misunderstood my silence as an inability to be consoled. He began to pry: "Did you know both of them?" When I said that I only really knew Dave—that we went to school together—I was trying to reassure him so he'd let me go: *It's okay*, I was trying to say, *I didn't know Evan, the victim, any better than you do; no need to worry about me.* But he took my answer as an opportunity for further encouragement. Finally, he must have felt he knew just what to say to lift my spirits: "After it happened, after he found him like that"—here his voice, low and confiding, cracked—"your friend, he carried his brother all the way to the hospital. By *himself.* Adrenaline's a funny thing. Or maybe it was God. Whatever it was, that little boy somehow found the strength to..."

He kept talking—I think he said Dave was a hero, that the fact that he was too late didn't change how heroically he'd acted—but I was barely listening. Mentally, I was barely even there. Most of me was with Dave. There he was, in the apartment, bloodied but standing up.

No, not the apartment. Cube City.

Cradling a body. Staring right at me.

Did I tell the cop what I was thinking?

Of course not. He'd never believe me.

I didn't want to believe me.

Why on earth would someone attempt to rescue the person they'd inflicted such violence upon?

I didn't and don't know.

Was he trying to cover his tracks? Was he capable of that sort of calculation?

Even if he was, there must have been better ways. Especially when there were no witnesses. Well, no witnesses who would talk.

Sometimes I imagine speaking to Dave's dad. We're in a

courtroom; he's under oath. "Are you telling the truth?" I ask him. "Is that what really happened?" But all he says is, "I love my boy," over and over. And I think: do I know the truth? Should I be telling it? Am I under oath too?

Maybe that's why I'm writing this story. Forget literary fiction: this whole story is better off as a courtroom drama. I'd have to add a few scenes here and there, but I could do it. I could have myself speak up to the cop, who would take my words seriously but nevertheless pat my head reassuringly. I could have a lawyer point out—in court? down at the station?—that there's not enough evidence to convict Dave. That even if he *did* kill his brother, he looked blameless in the eyes of the law. Self-defense—that's what it was.

I could have someone decree that there's no reason whatsoever to believe that they got the wrong man or that Dave's a threat in the future.

In fact, he or she could declare Dave, and everyone else, to be entirely exonerated.

Case closed.

I wouldn't have to suggest that the eyes of the law are blind, because I would still be a kid and kids don't talk in such a quippy manner, not in court or in (good) fiction.

Besides, just because Dave was capable of violence didn't mean his dad wasn't, right? Just the opposite was more likely. The violence I'd witnessed must've been learned somewhere, right? And the fact that the cops found Dave's father snoring drunkenly on the bloodied couch *was* damning, right? Despite my nagging desire to do so, there was and is no need to figure out when he got drunk—or why, after brutally murdering his son, he would neatly line up his work boots on the floor next to the couch and plop down for a snooze. Speaking of his boots: the fact that, according to news accounts, only the toes of the boots had left bloody prints all over the room was just that: a fact. Not a particularly relevant or telling detail. Certainly not a literary detail that demands to be read, analyzed, and interpreted. *Does that mean he was tiptoeing?* I tell myself to stop asking. *Why would he be tiptoeing unless he thought his boys were sleeping—alive and sleeping—in the other room?*

The tennis courts. Like I said, I wasn't there that day.

I'm almost sure of it.

But sometimes, sometimes I swear I *was*.

"Have a great fucking summer," I repeat.

"I remember it so clearly," I say.

"He didn't mean anything by it," I explain. "Really. He was just trying to be nice. Words didn't have the same limits for him as they did for the rest of us."

I can see it all so vividly: There's Ms. Tollackson, hustling away. There's Dave, grinning. (Does he have a full set of teeth? No, I suppose that's impossible. But his fake tooth is suctioned in so well that it looks real.)

And there I am, standing on the court with the others, biding my time until I can tell this story.

* * *

Discussion Questions

1. What is the point of retelling and embellishing stories about past experiences or colorful characters? Is it to entertain, to develop a narrative for our lives, or something else? What is the author's point for telling this story?

2. The author frequently questions the authenticity of his childhood memories. Do you think childhood memories change, and if so, what causes the change—for what purpose does our mind change memories?

3. In the story, the narrator writes, "*I remembers hearing Evan say, 'How many times do I have to tell you not to play my Nintendo?' But I'm starting to believe that this memory is false.*" Why would the narrator's memory (*or our own memories*) need to insert this kind of information into a memory fragment?

4. The narrator wants to remember that he spoke up on Dave's behalf when he was attacked by his brother and that he is the kind of person who speaks up for others. Even if he didn't actually speak up at the time, is there value in him falsely remembering that he did?

5. Do you have a clear childhood memory that, later as an adult, you questioned the truth of? Do you have a childhood memory that, as an adult, you evaluated differently from your older perspective? Explain.

* * *

The Zombie in the Bathroom

Maura Morgan

* * *

<u>Content Disclosure</u>: Horror Elements

* * *

My car protested this morning in the dark of January at my apartment. I couldn't blame it. With bone-chilling, midthirties cold, and rain coming down in buckets, it pelted automobile exteriors and skin with icy pins.

At five-thirty in the morning, wipers batting at the windshield to keep the sleet at bay, I drove to work. I slowly moved through the city and finally pulled into the parking lot at home base, where people emerged in front of my low beams, huddled beneath pine trees with cardboard boxes over their heads.

I never gave them much thought until Congress passed the Zombie Rights Act, and these humans went from being undead to a protected group and came out of hiding.

Not everyone becomes a zombie, just those with the right mix of recombinant chemicals in their system. Contrary to popular belief, zombies don't eat brains and aren't cannibals. Yes, they are undead and animated; some are cognizant and can speak. They rot away slowly as their bodies eat themselves, disappearing when the mottled flesh falls from their bones and their brains fully decompose. When they cannot move, they are taken into custody by a hospice group until they fully expire and can be laid to rest. Until then, they are untouchable, like any other resident of the US. I don't know if they know they are zombies, but I believe the undead realize they are different because of the glares and stares of the living, and their odor makes people gag.

They don't bother anyone. They just are. When the weather is pleasant, they spend their days wandering. When the weather is inclement, they find places to hole up until the rain stops.

Some zombies have absolutely nothing and lumber around with arms held stiffly at their side, dragging an uncooperative leg behind them, oblivious to the world. They step out in traffic; I've dodged them many times as I picked my way through the burbs into the city. I'm a ranger at a park at the confluence of three rivers. Other undead push shopping carts filled with sleeping bags or blankets and little trinkets gathered from the roadside and garbage cans, something to trade. Many hoard things because they remember having something. They teeter on the edge between awareness and disregard. They speak in lolled words, sometimes chasing thoughts to nowhere. Still, they never bother anyone.

We allow them to rest anywhere in the park they want at

night; it's a public space. The park isn't fenced in, and we can't chase them out. Each morning, we poke them into consciousness—as much as possible and make them move on. We must. If we don't, the living public complains and doesn't tolerate the zombies when they want to use the park.

I briskly treaded the brick path beneath an umbrella to the riverfront office to punch in for the day. My breath, hot from my lungs, swirled around my head. Despite being somewhat hungover and battling a cold, I felt quite alive today. My supervisor Mitch sat at his desk, warming his hands with coffee. Evan leaned against the office wall, hands stuffed in his parka pockets. We had a brief meeting about our day.

"It's going to be difficult," Mitch concluded. "The weather is against us."

I nodded and felt a sneeze coming on. I hurriedly reached into my jacket pocket for a tissue from my stash.

We expected few visitors due to the weather, but we must do our job. It's a directive from City Hall. No law on the books prevented it, but it's policy: no zombies in the park during daylight. Most days we don't have a problem. On bad days, they grumbled louder but still moved on.

Mitch unlocked the men's bathroom, I opened the ladies', and Evan unlocked the parking lot gate. Then, we unlocked the small turbine museum, walked the paths, picked up trash, and looked for anomalies in our morning hike. Nothing out of the ordinary, expected, given the nasty weather conditions. We knew where the zombies gathered and politely told them it was time to move on. Most didn't argue, and when they did, it was because they didn't understand. It's hard for some to process the meaning of no loitering when they've done it all night. It's hard for us to say the living don't want to see you; you make them uncomfortable, and we avoided being blunt. The zombies know their situation and don't need to be reminded. Most headed to the only places they can stay out of the weather: the shelters. Some protested, but we knew who they were, and most can be convinced it's for the best.

We herded them to the park exit, and they dispersed into the city with little trouble. One tried to take my umbrella, but it was a minor incident. We moved to the next task, but it will be a long day without our regular duties. None of us liked doing busy work.

Only the diehard visitors, the joggers and dog walkers, were out that morning, outfitted in appropriate gear. We saw them regardless of the weather, and they always blessed us with a muted wave as they passed.

When we finished, we headed back to the office. We hung our coats on the wrought iron wall hangers, and Mitch fired up the kerosene heater before settling in for a day of drudge work.

We weren't there for more than fifteen minutes when an elderly man knocked and opened the door, not waiting for a "come in." He was dressed in a Burberry wool coat, a brown plaid scarf, and an Irish tweed trilby hat with a leash over his arm. A miniature schnauzer was perfectly groomed and well-mannered at the end of the leash. He also carried a large, black golf umbrella. His nose was red. He closed the door behind him after a gust of wind banged it against the wall. Evan let go of the First Aid refresher book he was reading, and I looked up from the city map I'd been studying—I was new to the job, trying to familiarize myself with the area so that when visitors ask questions, I could answer intelligently.

"There's a zombie in the bathroom," he said indignantly. "He's locked himself in the handicap stall and won't come out."

"How do you know he's a zombie," Mitch asked, "and not another park patron using the facilities?"

"Because of the stench," the man withdrew a handkerchief from his coat pocket and gave a thunderous, snot-filled blow into it. "I have a terrible cold and can't smell soup or my aftershave, but I can smell him, and now I can't get it out of my nose. And, when I banged on the door to politely ask him to move on, all he did was grunt."

I glanced from Mitch to the man, wondering where the conversation would turn. Civility has disappeared in the last few years, and things sour fast, especially among the entitled. Mitch must keep things civil, even if this fellow had other ideas.

"I saw him go in on my way into the park to walk Duke here, and when I came back an hour later to use the facilities myself, he was still there."

"Thank you for letting us know, sir," Mitch said, pushing back on his wheeled chair and opening the door; he ushered the man outside. A few moments passed, and the man didn't move.

"Aren't you going to do something about it?"

"What do you suggest?" Mitch asked bravely, crossing his arms over his chest. My eyes widened at Mitch's brazenness. He's been here a few years and is used to dealing with demanding, living humans and dead people. Some situations, like the one now, have no easy answers. We know about the zombies; it's the people who run this state that seem to deny their existence and avoid addressing the "problem." We're always open to suggestions.

"Can't you call law enforcement and arrest him?" the man

asked.

"What has the zombie done? How has he broken the law?"

The man stumbled over his answer and finally sputtered a reply.

"Loitering," he said. "Yes, loitering."

"It's a park," Mitch reminded him. "When you stop and look at the scenery over the river, you loiter. When you pause to listen to the birds, you loiter. You loiter when you lie on a blanket in the sunshine to nap. Maybe he's just taking a breather."

I got the distinct feeling Mitch gave that reason before, and I hid my smirk, thinking *touché.*

"And maybe he's ruining the park experience for the rest of us." The man snorted. Mitch stared at him. "You really need to do something about it."

"I think you're better at doing something about it than me. Did you vote in the last election, sir?"

"You know I did. Straight ticket."

"Of course," Mitch said, scratching his beard with great thought. "I know, my superiors know, everyone in the park system knows this is a problem. It seems the only ones who don't know about this problem are the people who can do something about it. You should speak to your elected officials and complain to them. Better yet, maybe you should take an interest in these people, these zombies, and find out what they see as a solution to the problem."

The man gave Mitch a stern look, huffed, and left, sneezing on his way out.

"You're in trouble," Evan said with a grin.

"Come on," Mitch said with a scoop of his arm. "Let's go

see what's up with this guy."

I grabbed my coat, hat, and umbrella and followed Mitch and Evan into the men's bathroom.

Beneath the partition, I saw a pair of Reeboks and faded jeans, tattered and torn, frayed at the hems, and a ratty, stained blanket filled with tiny holes burned by cigarettes. The Reebok soles were splitting.

Based on Evan's and Mitch's expressions, the odor was ripe and rank. I couldn't smell it because of my cold. Tiny bits of skin and dried blood lay scattered on the cement floor.

"Sir," Mitch said, knocking gently on the stall door. Unintelligible grumbling followed Mitch's greeting. "Sir," he repeated, "I'm afraid you'll have to leave."

A phlegmy, guttural reply followed.

"Why?" It's what he asked, but it came out as a distortion of sound. I only understood because it was a reasonable question for him to ask.

"Because, sir," Mitch said, fumbling for a complete answer. "You can't stay here."

"Why not?"

The zombie's voice intensified, and he coughed. Mitch bit his lip; his only valid response is because the zombie is interfering with living park patrons, possibly creating a health hazard in the facilities, and potentially, unintendedly, making an awful mess we'd have to clean up if he expires. We can't catch the zombie condition, but the smell was enough to make Mitch and Evan gag.

"Come out, and we'll take you to the shelter."

"Can't, dammit. More'n ninety days. Smell too bad."

The door opened, and a jogger came in to use the urinal. He screwed up his face seeing us standing at the handicap stall. He heard the movement inside the stall and shook his head.

"Christ!" He grunted and ran out.

Mitch yanked his head toward the outer door, silently asking Evan and me to follow him out.

We stepped into the cold January air as the hydraulic door closer hissed and squeaked, gently shutting behind us.

I tugged at my knit cap to resettle it upon my head and blew on my hands to warm them.

"It's nasty in there!" Evan exclaimed. "Nobody's going to use that bathroom. No amount of air freshener will get that stink out. What if he expires in there, and we're left cleaning up the mess?"

"We're going to have to call law enforcement, you know," Mitch said, folding his arms, rocking back and forth on his heels as he looked over the juncture of the rivers from the viewing platform. Though the cold lingered, the rain stopped. I knew he was right.

"Technically," I said, "he's not doing anything wrong."

Mitch and Evan sighed in unison.

"I'll talk to law enforcement," Mitch finally said.

"I'll talk to the zombie," I said. "See if I can reason with him."

Evan opted to patrol the path and let other visitors know the men's bathroom was temporarily closed. I inhaled as deep as I could without coughing before I headed back into the yellow concrete half of the building that is the men's facility. I resigned myself to what could be a long wait and a difficult conversation as I plopped on the concrete floor outside the stall. I leaned my umbrella against the wall. The floor was cold, solid, and damn uncomfortable, even for my generous butt cheeks and insulated parka under me. The only sound was an erratic drip from a nearby faucet. I made a mental note to get that fixed.

"My supervisor's gone to call law enforcement," I said, drawing my knees up to my chest because the cold had already seeped through my khaki pants and thermals. I heard the zombie shuffling around in the stall and glanced beneath the partition again. He changed position and was lying on his side on the floor. I couldn't see his face. I tapped my foot nervously, simultaneously wondering if I should just be quiet or try to strike up a conversation—reason with him. I didn't want to make him angry. "What's your name?"

The zombie grunted, and I thought he wanted to answer me. A long pause passed before he did.

"John S'ith," he replied. He was hard to understand because his voice is obstructed, and he gurgles a lot. I tried not to ponder why. Instead, I wondered if John Smith was his name or a bad attempt at an alias. He put my curiosity to rest and told me people called him Jake.

"Can I call you Jake?" I asked.

"Sure."

"I'm Chad. Sorry, we need you to leave."

He confessed that he just came in to get out of the rain. Said there's nothing worse than being in the rain, that his skin sheds faster. He knows he's a zombie.

"I understand," I said, banishing the thought of skin shedding in clumps like melting ice cream. But I brought the idea back, as repulsed as I was. I realized I had a lot of questions. "Does it hurt? Jake? When the rain hits your skin?"

Not physically, just mentally, he said.

"Mentally?"

Then I suddenly understood. I don't know much about zombies, but watching your skin fall off in a downpour would be unsettling.

"Hmmm. Does the cold bother you?"

Jake moved around again and soon sat beside me with the partition between us. His hand rested on the floor, at the end of a red and blue flannel shirt sleeve. His hand was black and blue and filled with indentations. He was missing a couple of fingertips; the bare bones were showing.

He said no, just the rain. Even the snow wasn't a problem; it just prolonged their—

His words trailed off, but I filled in the blank. Final death.

"We don't get much snow here," I said. I saw the puffs of breath coming from my mouth. I coughed, feeling my own congestion worsening. I needed Sudafed.

The conversation turned dark when Jake spoke. He told me he and other zombies had been bussed here from up north.

"Bussed here?"

"Cincinnati," Jake said. He went on to say the living in Cincinnati don't tell the zombies where they're being taken. His voice took on an echo of anger despite his speech impediment. "They don't tell us this, 'ut we aren't stu'id. They're ho'ing the warrer tem'eratures will ex'edite..."

Hoping warmer temperatures will expedite their—there's those words again—final death. I cringed at the thought of my fellow living human beings treating these poor souls like they were disposable.

I shifted uncomfortably on my buttocks, ashamed people

can be so heartless. No one wants to confront this problem, so they pass it on.

"How long have you been this way?"

"A year," he said, coughing, his mouth filling with phlegm and detritus. His voice turned raspy as he told me he didn't want to be a burden on his family.

"They couldn't 'ear to see me this way, so I left." He hacked, and I sensed from the bodily noises coming from the other side his expectorant was juicy. I heard him spit into the toilet. "Shit," he said like his mouth was full of marbles.

I reached into my jacket pocket for some tissues and passed them beneath the partition. I appreciated Jake understood he was witnessing his own slow decay. I didn't know whether he wanted to speed it up or slow it down. I also appreciated he didn't want to spit lung or stomach tissue onto the floor. He still had a sense of consideration.

He didn't immediately take the tissue from me, so I waved it in case he didn't see it.

His fingers grazed mine, and I couldn't help but recoil, swiftly withdrawing my hand. He spat again, prolonged and with force. The tissue plopped into the toilet, and the whoosh of flushing water followed.

He wanted to know if he'd be arrested, and, given this was my first encounter with a zombie in this way, I didn't know.

I sighed heavily.

"I wish I could say no, but they might physically remove you. Is there any way I can convince you it's in your best interest to leave before law enforcement gets here?"

"I not a criminal," Jake said. "Just got nowhere safe to 'e."

I understood. The living don't realize how hard it is, that

Jake didn't choose to be a zombie, and he was just looking for a place out of the weather.

"What can I do to help?" I asked. I could give him money, but what would that accomplish?

I heard Jake moving again, and after a bit of a struggle, he reached his feet. He picked up the blanket with his feet firmly planted on the cement floor. I stood, too, wondering what Jake was thinking and what he would do.

A moment later, the latch slid, and the door opened. I braced for what I was about to see because I'd never been this close to a zombie. I always saw them from a comfortable distance—through the barricade of my mind, if necessary, if I saw them at all. Most people looked away from zombies when they encountered them. To ease their discomfort, the living tossed spare change their way, like that would help. I'd been doing this job for nearly three months now and hadn't had the courage to look any of them in the eye. Guilt, I supposed, stopped me.

I swallowed hard and clenched my fingers. My body stiffened in preparation for what I was about to see. I did a quick scan of Jake's presence. At about six feet, he was the same height as me; his hair was patchy, and its remnants were salt and pepper. He was mature; I put him around forty-five or so. He was athletic, which told me why he'd survived this long. Even with my stuffy nose, I expected to be hit dead on with a fetid, foul smell, but I wasn't.

Surprisingly enough, it was Jake's attempt at a smile I noticed next. A missing eyeball left a gaping hole covered by a thin veil of eyelid in its socket, and random pieces of flesh were missing from his face. His lips were raw and nearly nonexistent.

Blackened gums and rotting teeth were exposed. No wonder he had trouble speaking. Usually, a smile would only be evident with the accompanying facial muscles. But I could tell he was smiling. There were crinkles around his eyes communicating this to me, and in that moment, I wish I'd known him before he became... this.

But I was puzzled.

"Why'd you come out?" I blurted. "Was it the idea of getting arrested?"

Jake glanced to the floor and pretended to adjust the blanket slung over his forearm.

He said something then that I still remember.

"It's a lonely path to death, being in the world alone. There aren't many people," he paused, "taking the time to talk to people like me."

I barely heard him. With chunks of flesh freshly expelled from his system, his voice had gone raspier. Each word was quiet and garbled. I understood the importance of lips in communication.

He stepped out of the stall and stopped.

"You did. That 'eans a lot."

Now I was ashamed and could barely look him in his one good eye.

"Thank you." He gently touched my arm with his pitted, decaying hand. That time, I didn't cringe.

"You know," I said, "there's a picnic shelter by the river. It's not as cozy as the bathroom, but it will keep the rain off you. No one uses it on cold and rainy days. Oh, and," I said, handing Jake my umbrella, "take this. It might help."

He took it and nodded, and I pulled open the door for

him, watching him as he left and disappeared steadily down the trail. I was still pondering Jake's existence when Mitch breathlessly approached me from the opposite direction. On his heels were two city police officers, their faces red and chests heaving. We could all use a mandatory cardio regimen. They bypassed me and ran into the men's bathroom. I waited for them, allowing Mitch to discover Jake's absence for himself.

Moments later, Mitch reappeared at my side, still trying to catch his breath. His eyes were watering, and I could only imagine it was from the stench in the bathroom. Thank God for my cold.

"Where'd he go?"

I shrugged, looking past Mitch down the trail.

"He moved on."

"Good," Mitch said, "let's hope he doesn't come back."

I didn't answer him because I hoped to see Jake again, even without a cold.

* * *

Discussion Questions

1. Should the zombies in the story have the same rights as living people? What are the factors you are considering in developing your answer?

2. The living people in the story have created laws excluding zombies from places they might visit (*like the park during the day*) because it makes the living uncomfortable seeing them. Do people have the right to be protected from seeing other people (*or things*) that make them uncomfortable?

3. If the zombie could speak and think but was rude and somewhat aggressive (*but not dangerous*), would your opinion be different about which rights zombies are entitled to? If so, why (*or why not*)?

4. If you were the narrator in the story and encountered John Smith (*the zombie*) in the bathroom, what would you have done?

5. One interpretation of the story is the zombies are an allegory for the way society treats the homeless. In what ways do you see parallels and differences in the way the two groups should be treated? What (*if anything*) is the basis/cause for the differences?

* * *

Bingo Was His Name-O

Bradley Greenburg

* * *

<u>**Content Disclosure**</u>: Terminal Illness

* * *

Lorraine finally calls after three hours at the animal hospital.

"The X-ray doesn't show the color of the plastic."

"It was the frisbee. I'm telling you." Our son, eight years old, is pantomiming a ball. "Max thinks it was a tennis ball." I shake my head, wave at him to leave it. "I knew he was too quiet back there." I cover the receiver and whisper, *She says it's plastic.* "What's the prognosis?"

"That's the bad news."

"What was the good news?"

"That it was plastic and not metal. Or a battery. Or glass."

"Not sure that qualifies as good—"

"Eight hundred and seventy-five dollars."

I collapse onto the couch. Max's expression jump cuts from anxiety to fear. He bolts to his room.

"You've got to be shitting me. He was a *rescue*."

"*Is* a rescue. I don't think the moral equation is part of the financial equation."

"It should be..."

I can't stop imagining what almost nine hundred dollars will buy. So many things that don't eat other things, that don't require healthcare.

"Are you still there?"

"Yeah. I was thinking."

"Well, think fast. They need a decision."

"What are the chances he'll just be fine?"

"Peter."

"Dogs are always eating things. Ask what the odds are he'll shit it out and be fine."

"I'm not asking the vet for odds."

"Percentage, then."

"She's a serious doctor, Pete. It's not airfare or a refi. There's a life at stake here."

"A dog's life."

"Go tell your son that."

"It would be better if we closed ranks now. We'll say he had a procedure for, say, a believable one-fifty. Which, for the record, I'm willing to pay. Then, if he shits gold, we're golden. And if he succumbs to his injur—"

"Dies, you mean."

"If that happens, then we just explain to Max that we did all we could, etc."

"Et cetera?"

"Anguish, worry... I don't know. Duress?"

"He'll see through it."

Max returns to the kitchen, raises his eyebrows. He's given us as long as it should take grown-ups to magically sort out a life-and-death issue. I offer my weariest shrug.

"Max is here, honey. Anyway, I'm glad the vet thinks he'll be okay. See you in a few."

I hang up. I don't think Lorraine will plunk down nearly a grand without my acquiescence. My passive-aggressive effort to settle the matter is also a tacit acceptance of responsibility for the consequences, which I put at about fifty percent. I'm not sure how that translates to odds.

Max's fingers are crossed. Both hands. "What did mom say?"

"Good news, bad news."

"Oh no, is—"

Max starts to tear up.

"Hey, it's good news, buddy. The vet is taking care of it."

"Is it an operation? How many days until he can come home?" He isn't any less afraid.

"It's a quick procedure. Mom will bring him home pretty soon."

He screws up his face, and I can tell we're about to switch subjects to something he knows about from TV or one of his friends.

"How can they do it so fast? It's an operation, right?"

I hand him a Kleenex.

"No. See, the vet explained it to Mom, and she ran me through it."

He scrutinizes me for signs of bullshit. I'm glad I have to lie a lot at work.

"They have this machine that creates very powerful

suction. What's the name of that vacuum cleaner you're always admiring at Costco?"

"The Dyson Cinetic Big Ball?"

"Yeah. It's made by Dyson."

"Whoa. I had no idea they made veterinary equipment."

It's hard to stay on task with the intense rush of pride I experience in my son's use of the word "veterinary," which I know my wife's sister's kids would never come up with.

"They do, and it's amazing. Apparently. I mean, I haven't seen it."

"Does it have the ball?"

"The what now?"

"The ball. I'm guessing it doesn't since there are no maneuverability issues."

Maneuverability. Are you kidding me? You think Rhonda and Keith's kids are learning *that* at Montessori?

"Mom didn't say, but I could hear it whirring. It was impressive."

"And it just sucks out whatever is in the dog's stomach?"

"Or cat. I don't know if it works on smaller animals."

At work, I've learned that misdirection is crucial in concocting a story people believe. No one suspects a liar of going to so much trouble, which is understandable, since most liars are also lazy.

"Wouldn't it hurt? I mean, the plastic is rough from the biting and chewing, and then it travels back up his throat."

Max starts to get emotional again. I can appreciate his vivid imagination. It's something I cultivate in him whenever I can.

"I forgot to mention. They give him a pill first that softens any plastic material in the digestive system."

Max wipes away a tear. Though it's almost his bedtime, I pull a Mexican Coke out of the fridge and pour it unequally into two glasses over ice to take the sting out of the carbonation. It's a dirty trick. We almost never let him drink soda. Such a treat in a period of *duress*, whether his mother likes it or not, is almost certain to redirect his attention.

Max savors his cane sugar sweetened cola. "Before it reaches the duodenum?"

"I'm sure that's the case." I can't help myself. "*Duodenum*. Impressive, Max. How do you know the parts of the throat in such detail?"

"Actually, it's part of the small intestine. On the other side of the stomach."

"How do you know so much—"

"It was in a doctor show I watched."

I say, "Cheers," and we clink glasses. Everything is going to be fine.

"Poor Bingo," I offer. "Bingo was his name-o."

Max is crying.

"Bingo *is* his name-o."

* * *

Discussion Questions

1. Would Peter (*the father*) be right to lie to his son and tell him they tried to save the dog's life, even if they don't spend the money? To what extent should money be a factor in the decision-making process at all?
2. Under what circumstances is it appropriate and inappropriate to lie to a child, and what (*if any*) are the different factors that change the equation?
3. What should Peter do if his son insists on going to the veterinarian's office to wait during the promised surgery (*which might not be happening*)?
4. Is Peter right in making up the procedure details and making it sound as simple and painless as possible?
5. When (*if ever*) should Peter tell his son the truth about what really happened with Bingo's outcome and (*potential*) procedure?

* * *

Guilt-Edge Security

James A. Hartley

* * *

<u>Content Disclosure</u>: None

* * *

I sat beside the bar, rubbing my glass across polished mahogany and watching the trails of moisture it left behind. It must have cost them a fortune to ship real wood way out to the Rim. It didn't look synthetic. I looked over at the barman, and he tossed his head, then went back to polishing the glasses. Real authentic stuff. I was nursing my fourth bourbon when the guy walked in.

He was a florid, heavyset guy, and I could just tell he was a salesman. He had the suit, he had the haircut, and he had the little case. Maybe things would have been different if it had been a different night.

He swaggered up to the bar and planted himself like he owned the place. Maybe he did. He raised two fingers, and the barman filled a glass with what looked like scotch. He drained the first one quickly, then signaled for another. When his second arrived, he turned to scan the bar. I studied him out of the corner of my eye. Finally, he turned and looked at me, nodded then smiled. Another quick circuit of the room, and he slid his drink down the bar toward me.

"Hey, Mac," he said to me. "Mind if I join you?"

I shrugged and motioned to the place beside me. Looking back, that might have been the big mistake.

"You're in the game, right?" he said. "You look like the sort. Marketing and sales, right? No other reason for being out in this backwater. Let me guess. You're from Earth." I nodded, and he grinned.

"Yeah, me too. Jack. Jack Davis's the name." He thrust a meaty paw toward me, and I shook it.

"Steve Walker," I said.

"So, what are you drinking, Steve?" he said. I pointed at my bourbon, and he motioned to the barman and pointed to both our glasses. I didn't mind. If this Jack Davis was going to buy me drinks, I could put up with a pitch. I guessed that was what was coming. If I listened, he'd probably buy me drinks all night. I wouldn't have to sign anything, and I'd walk away at the end several bourbons better off.

"Well, Steve, it's lucky I ran across you. You and me being in the same game, you'll understand what I'm talking about. Let me ask you a question, Steve. What do you think about integrity?"

It was a funny sort of question.

"How do you mean?"

"Well, you know, you and me both, we're in sales. Is integrity a part of that?"

"I still don't..."

"Okay, maybe I need to make it a bit clearer. You ever hear of a place called Galipienzo?" I pressed my lips together and shook my head. He nodded. "Yeah, well, neither had I. Then I sort of bumped into the place. You know how it is."

I nodded my head to humor him and glanced significantly at my glass. He grinned and waved the barman over.

"The way I got involved was pretty simple," he said. "I'd been doing the Rim, selling a line of high-tech components to the emerging markets. Some of those Rim worlds had a lot of promise at the time. The returns were meager, but you have to have vision in this game. Am I right?" I nodded and looked attentive. The bourbon was good.

"You sell them a bit of tech, they build on that, then they start wanting bigger and better things. It was a good market, or, at least, it had the potential to be.

"I was just on the verge of getting somewhere with my collection of Rim worlds when I ran into Galipienzo. I got too greedy, I suppose. Wanted to add one more sleeper to the list. I didn't know too much about the place at the time. It had all the right criteria, out on the Rim, fairly isolated, not in the commercial mainstream. I thought it would be easy. Maybe if I'd gotten there about two centuries earlier. Oh, I did business there, good business, but in a place like Galipienzo, good business takes time."

I was starting to wonder if this was a pitch after all. The things Davis was saying made sense. I knew what it was like out there at the hard edge on the Rim.

"The thing about doing business in a society like that is, you've got to be able to work the hierarchies. That takes patience. I had to grease the right palms, get to know the connections and the faces. That led me to other names and faces. Gradually, my network started to grow. Word of mouth is the best sales tool you can get, right?"

"Yeah, don't I know it," I said. "That's why we're out here pounding the beat, winning their confidence."

"Right, Steve," said Davis. "Well, the Galipienzans were a cautious lot—always looking for the sting. That drew the process out. I was there maybe two, three months in all. Long enough to work out how the place worked, long enough to know that the only way I was going to do real business was with the Lord himself. Now, that's only a title, Steve. He's not a deity or anything, though he might as well have been. Sheesh, if you could've seen the guy..."

I smiled. I'd known a few like that in my time.

"Anyway, one of the first things I learned about the Galipienzans was that they liked to *own* things. It didn't matter what, but property was status. One way to own things was to dispossess your fellow natives. If they ran out of fellow Galipienzans, they looked elsewhere. Most of the other worlds didn't like them very much. I didn't like them very much— arrogant, sneering, opinionated bastards, and that's their good side. It meant they weren't very good at doing business. They couldn't market themselves, you see. That's where I came into the picture.

"Kayzoro, the Lord, had a product, but he didn't have anyone to market it for him. He knew he couldn't rely on his fellow Galipienzans to go out and have any chance of success. The only way he was going to achieve the status he desired was to own as much as he could of the known worlds. The only way to do that was to take out rights on the basic integrity of a few key individuals—possession by proxy."

Suddenly, I was confused again. I had no idea what he was talking about, but the man was buying my drinks, so I persisted.

"What do you mean by rights on integrity, Jack? I don't see how that factors in."

Davis sipped at his scotch and put down his glass. He ran his fingers through the beaded moisture on its side, then turned and fixed me with a serious expression.

"Listen, Steve," he said after a pause. "You have every right to ask that question. What place is there for integrity... say, call it a person's soul... in the hard-nosed reality of these days of FTL travel? It's true, the known universe is no longer what it used to be, and we don't believe in the sort of stuff we used to. Occasionally, I tell people to take the time to browse for a definition of *soul*. 'Don't let me stop you,' I tell them. I'm sure you'll find the answers. The accumulated knowledge of generations is at your fingertips."

"Yeah, and—"

"I guess what I'm saying is that I believe in integrity. In other words, I believe in souls, but maybe not in the way others think about them. It's a question of morality. For me, the soul is about having the ability to choose, to make your own decisions based upon your own understanding of what's right and wrong. Take away that right from someone, that freedom to choose, and you own his or her *soul* or whatever you want to call it. It took me a long time to understand that. By the time I realized that, it was too late—too late for me and too late for a lot of others."

I was starting to think I'd run into a religious nut, and any moment, he was going to come out with the pamphlets. But I was interested now, and the muzzy bourbon effect was softening my tolerance.

"Okay, Steve," he said. "Look around. Look at all the worlds out there. Sure, these worlds have elective processes, but behind all that, there's always someone who ultimately pulls the strings. You think these guys have souls, free will? They might have had once. Have you noticed how most of the big industrialists and people like that seem to have been around for a long, long time? The only way they've managed to do that is to lose part of themselves. I know how. I know exactly how they've managed to do it. They've given up the freedom to choose. Someone else calls the shots for them. Now, in my book, if they don't have that freedom, they've lost what we could loosely call their *soul*."

"So, what are you telling me, Jack?" I asked. "Is this some sort of religious spiel? You going to save my soul?"

"No, no. Sorry, Steve," he said. "Here, let me get you another drink." He motioned for the barman. "I'm getting a little ahead of myself."

The barman filled our glasses, and Davis stared down at them, then nodded and waited for the barman's retreat before continuing. He traced a pattern on the bar surface, pursed his lips, and then turned.

"Let me fill you in on Galipienzo. It might start to make more sense."

I took another sip at my bourbon—my sixth or seventh. I'd lost count.

"Galipienzo started small, but as a world, it had all the ingredients to make it something great. It sat isolated on the Rim for decades, a backwater overlooked by the trading communities and mainstream commerce around it. The world could have smoldered and sparked, then flared back into nonexistence, ignored by the rest of humanity, but Galipienzo had something special. You see, they had their own little scientific community. It interacted with the rest of the research community, but somehow they were on their own."

I'd seen worlds like that myself, but I still didn't see where this was going.

"What Galipienzo had to keep them apart was unique. The world was home to a tiny molecular structure." Davis held up his thumb and forefinger and peered through the gap between them. "That structure became known to the Galipienzan research community, and the beauty of it was that it defied analysis unless you knew how. That was their great discovery—how to analyze the stuff. They weren't going to tell anyone else how to do it.

"They worked out they had a good thing going as soon as they found out how to apply their little compound. As far as anyone can work out, it's the only means of producing the gene repressor that controls longevity. Think about it. I mean, really think about it. Do you understand the implications?"

I nodded and licked my lips.

"So, what did they do? They bottled the stuff, of course. Called it *Life*. A great name, don't you think? Beautiful marketing strategy. I wish I'd thought of it."

"So, if they've got this stuff, why haven't I seen it?" I asked him. "I would've thought it'd be all over the marketplace."

"You would have thought so, wouldn't you? But it didn't work like that. They had this stuff for, say, about three hundred years before it hit the broader byways. Think about it. You have an isolated community, and suddenly, it has access to this stuff that prolongs life span by a factor of three, four, or five. What happens? First, the population expands at an amazing rate. More people, longer life span, natural selection steps in. What's a life here or there along the way? People became disposable resources. Hell of an environment to grow up in.

"For a couple of hundred years, that worked admirably. They got on with their business, and we got on with ours. That was until Kayzoro clawed his way to the top of the heap. Finally, the Galipienzans had someone in charge who wasn't satisfied with his own little piece of real estate. The problem was, this guy was not just your run-of-the-mill expansionist head case. He was smart. He had that unusual combination of brains and strength.

"I told you how they like to own things. Kayzoro knew Galipienzo had its limitations. What was it—some small hick planet out in the sticks? He knew that if some tin-pot nation suddenly started going military, he'd have all of the combined forces of the known worlds down on him in less time than you could say 'response force.' Whatever else, you have to admire him for his smarts."

Davis leaned back and sighed. "Personally, I can't stand him. Nasty piece of work... Anyway, where was I? Oh yes, he had a far better way of conquering civilization. He had the ready-made tool at his fingertips. He had *Life*."

The bells of opportunity were ringing faintly in the back of my head, even through the bourbon haze.

"So, what's your involvement?" I asked.

Davis shrugged. "I'd been working the Galipienzan

market for some time, and finally, I managed to work my way up to Kayzoro himself. Oh, he wanted some of what I had to sell, no trouble there. It was just how he paid me. If only I'd had the foresight to see what was going on then. He knew exactly what he was doing. After that, *I* didn't have any choice. What would you have done in my position? There I was, and he was offering me the chance of a lifetime—literally. He paid me for my first consignment in *Life*. By the time we got to the third, I was hooked. It was then that he made me an offer, and how could I refuse? There it was, guaranteed income and my own personal supply direct from the source."

He took a deep swallow from his drink. "He used me to hook a few of the others in over time. We're all in the same game, after all. We talk, compare notes, swap war stories. It was easy enough to do. I guess, in a way, we do business despite rather than because of him. We act as our own little support network. Regardless, you've got to have faith in the product to do good business. That's how it works. And I've certainly got faith in the product. As for job security, there's nothing to beat it."

"So why didn't you tell him to stuff his product? Why didn't you just demand payment?"

He looked at me for a long time before answering.

"When you get to a certain age, your mortality begins to tell. You've felt it, Steve. You start to slow down, feel the strain, become less enthusiastic. You start to think about how long you've got left and what you have left to do. How can you seriously pass up an opportunity like that? You can't. You'd sell your own soul for the chance to escape that terminus—anyone would. And that applies just as much to your leading industrialists and power brokers across the known worlds. You see why I was talking about souls before? Kayzoro knew that, and he knew the power it could give him. Just imagine the prospect of having within the palm of your hand the means to deny death. What would you give to have that power? He knew he had me."

I nodded slowly.

Davis continued looking at me intently.

"Remember how I asked you about integrity?"

"Uh-huh."

"Well, the truth of it is, I never had any intention of compromising my integrity; you have to understand that. When it came to it, I didn't have much choice. Doing business across multiple worlds can be a hell of a task at the best of times, but with Kayzoro calling the shots, it was really difficult. Integrity just didn't come into it. I suppose I could have had a choice, but he owned me by then. What could I do?"

Davis retrieved his case from the floor, flipped it open, and reached inside.

"Look at me," he said without looking at me. "How old do you think I am? Forty? Fifty? Well, I'll tell you. Two hundred and six next birthday."

I almost dropped my glass.

Davis smiled and nodded slowly. "Anyway, I've been talking to you for too long." He reached into the case and pulled something out. "Here, let me leave you with this. It's just a sampler of our new product line. We call it *Rejuve*. Cute little bottle. See the way it glows? That one's yours to keep."

"Um, thanks," I said, looking down at the small glass tube lying in my hand.

Davis got to his feet. "Well, it's been good to meet you, Steve. I'll see you next time I'm through this way—in about eight years. We'll talk some more then. You'll be here."

He nodded to the barman and walked out.

That was eight years ago to the day. Now I'm sitting in that same bar. Maybe if I'd realized what a good pitch it was, things would have been different. But I didn't, and I'm sitting watching the door, hoping he'll show. There's a half-full glass of bourbon on the bar beside me and a small, empty bottle in my hand.

* * *

This story is a part of our legacy-of-excellence program, first printed in the After Dinner Conversation—May 2021 issue.

Discussion Questions

1. If you were in the narrator's position, would you drink the bottle of *Rejuve* that was handed to you?
2. Assuming you did drink the bottle of *Rejuve* and it did work as advertised, would you be back for more of it eight years later?
3. What would change about the way you live your life if you knew you were going to live 400 or 500 years?
4. Does the threat of impending death affect how you live your life? In what way? Does knowing you have a limited amount of time make each day and each choice more precious? Would a nearly unlimited life span spoil that preciousness and urgency?
5. Kayzoro believed that if too many people knew they had discovered *Life* they would be invaded for their resource. Do you agree? How is this pattern similar or different compared to a country on Earth that discovers an abundance of a limited resource, like oil or diamonds?

* * *

Author Information

Disconnect

Julia Meinwald is a writer of fiction and musical theatre and a gracious loser at a wide variety of board games She has stories published or forthcoming in *Bayou Magazine, Vol 1. Brooklyn, West Trade Review, VIBE,* and *The Iowa Review*, among others. Her work as a composer has been heard in productions across the US and in Canada, and the cast album for her musical *The Magnificent Seven* streams on various platforms. *www.juliameinwaldwrites.com*; *https://linktr.ee/juliameinwald*

Room 101

J.B. Polk is Polish by birth, a citizen of the world by choice. Her first story was short-listed for the *Irish Independent*/Hennessy Awards, Ireland, 1996. Since she went back to writing fiction in 2020, 74 of her stories, flash fiction and nonfiction, have been accepted for publication. She has recently won 1st prize in the International Human Rights Arts Movement literary contest. X (Twitter) *@jbtrans2006*; Facebook *@jolanta.polk*

The Compelled

Z.D. Dochterman writes speculative fiction and teaches in the Writing Program at USC. His essays have appeared in *The Conversation, Salon,* and *The Houston Chronicle,* among other publications. He also co-hosts a weekly creative writing workshop for formerly incarcerated people in Los Angeles. X (Twitter) *@zddochterman*

The Lives and Time of David Hackman

Patrick Hueller writes and teaches in Minnesota. He's against instant replay in sports, but for it in life.

The Zombie in The Bathroom

Maura Morgan is a writer of both fiction and nonfiction, covering a range of topics, including travel, history, speculative and historical fiction, and short stories. She graduated from Drexel University with a Master of Fine Arts degree in Creative Writing. She is working on a historical novel. X (Twitter) *@maura0718*; Substack *@maura0718*; Facebook *@maura0718*

Bingo Was His Name-O

Bradley Greenburg is the author of the novel *When Lilacs Last in the Dooryard Bloomed* (Sandstone Press, UK: 2014). He teaches Shakespeare, film, and creative writing at Northeastern Illinois University in Chicago. He has published recent work at PopMatters. *www.bradleygreenburg.com;* X (Twitter) *@BGinCHI*

Guilt-Edge Security

James A. Hartley is an Australian author now based in Germany by way of the UK. Although an occasional poet, his primary focus has always been short fiction. He feels that it is there that the author is naked on the page and that in the short story, there really is nowhere to hide. His works have appeared in Australia, Canada, the USA and been translated into both Greek and Italian.

Additional Information

Reviews

If you enjoyed reading these stories, please consider doing an online review. It's only a few seconds of your time, but it is very important in continuing the series. Good reviews mean higher rankings. Higher rankings mean more sales and a greater ability to release stories.

Print Books

https://www.afterdinnerconversation.com

Purchase our growing collection of print anthologies, "Best of," and themed print book collections. Available from our website, online bookstores, and by order from your local bookstore.

Podcast Discussions/Audiobooks

https://www.afterdinnerconversation.com/podcastlinks

Listen to our podcast discussions and audiobooks of After Dinner Conversation short stories on Apple, Spotify, or wherever podcasts are played. Or, if you prefer, watch the podcasts on our YouTube channel or download the .mp3 file directly from our website.

Patreon

https://www.patreon.com/afterdinnerconversation

Get early access to short stories and ad-free podcasts. New supporters also get a free digital copy of the anthology *After Dinner Conversation– Season One*. Support us on Patreon!

Book Clubs/Classrooms

https://www.afterdinnerconversation.com/book-club-downloads

After Dinner Conversation supports book clubs! Receive free short stories for your book club to read and discuss!

Social

Connect with us on Facebook, YouTube, Instagram, TikTok, Substack, and Twitter.

Special Thanks

After Dinner Conversation gratefully acknowledges the support of the following individuals and organizations.

* * *

In Alphabetical Order

Anonymous, Marie Anderson, Ria Bruns, Brett Clark, Jarvis Coffin, Rebecca Dueben, Tina Forsee, Deb Gain-Braley, David Gibson, Ron Koch, Sandra Kolankiewicz, Donna Lormand, Anja Peerdeman, John Sheirer, David Shultz, Frank Strada, Mitchell Sweet, and Bill Weston.

* * *

Donation Information

Please send your 501(c)(3) donations to:

After Dinner Conversation

2516 S. Jentilly Lane, Tempe, AZ 85282

https://www.afterdinnerconversation.com/donation

https://www.patreon.com/afterdinnerconversation

Milton Keynes UK
Ingram Content Group UK Ltd.
UKHW011143220424
441551UK00007B/793